The Life of Almost

With
love,
Anna Vaughan
May, 2019.

X

The Life of Almost

Anna Vaught

First published as a paperback edition by Patrician Press 2018

British Library Cataloguing in Publication Data. A catalogue record for this book is available from the British Library.

ISBN paperback edition 978-1-9997030-2-8

Published by Patrician Press 2018

For more information: www.patricianpress.com

For Julie, Stephen, James and Alex. Love forever.

When I was a kid, Lewis took his own life.
I heard them say he took it, but where it went,
I couldn't say or wasn't told. Perhaps it had
been drained, in The Sloop, with all his pints,
or thrown gladly off Stack Rocks with a shout
that he married well and was a man they liked,
but I don't know. For once, though I was very young,
I saw a look from out the corner of his eye as he
shipped off, went laughing with a pot boy and a girl:
that look it said, I think, that Lewis wanted rescuing,
but no-one came, as the sea foam danced in
Cardigan Bay.
Almost Llewhellin. 'Lewis'.

'…A tall tree on the river's bank, one half of it
burning from root to top, the other half in green leaf.'
Peredur Son Of Efrawg (from The Mabinogi).

A grave at Capel Dewi, Broad Haven: In Loving Memory of Almost Derian Llewhellin of Druidstone Haven. Presumed lost at sea, with his beloved wife, Seren Davies Llewhellin, of Clandestine Quay, May 1963.

1

Almost comes to tell me a story

A dreary, dry Sunday afternoon
Far from the sea coast.
Stifled; sick; quiet in the wrong way.
Border country.

Stiff-backed and wondering. The back of my house had blown dark and everything was ill. And yet… oh it was a mass of muddling things: we had everything before us, we had nothing before us, we were all going direct to heaven, we were all going the other way: I wanted to be sure I had the spring of hope in the season of darkness, but these I could not distinguish.

So. This is when you need a story.

Would *he* come to me if I sent for him now?

And *would he come to me*, if I asked for him?

My beautiful friend. Blazing paradox, he was.

Yes, I knew he would come to me if I summoned him. He was someone I hadn't seen in a long time. Someone no-one had seen in a long time and he was different. He had a sort of indeterminate form—ah, glorious; triumphant. He moved through building and garden as if there were no boundaries for him. His whole world was a little room for him to loll in and all of time a place to walk in, as he pleased. And I thought that he could help me, tired of life as I was. Yes, I thought he would be able to help. I needed to listen to his story and I wanted to write it down and give it to you, whoever you might be.

A knock at the door.

Boy come up from Pembrokeshire. Or off-world. I don't know. Somewhere else, and fine.

'Oh, it is dark in here, but we can do something about that.'

Hello, Almost—it is so good to see you.

He brought some coastal light in with him, this beautiful man, and the growls and whines of now-world were silenced and so I said, *Almost, please tell me a story. I am so jaded. I feel sad.*

'But does it need to be a happy story?'

No, Almost: the life and happiness are in the telling and in the beauty of your words.

And he began by telling me who we would meet along the way and how it would change me and let me get to know him better. And that I would come to understand that death and its precincts instruct us just as much as life.

2

Almost's World and Almost tells a tale

Are you listening? These are the people you are going to meet. I'm making it a bit old fashioned, but then you and I do not naturally co-exist. Here we are, then; it's a table of contents.

Almost, I'm listening.

So, then: Almost. The protagonist and teller of this story. Well, that's me.

Perfection. She was my sister and her name didn't suit her. I loved her, though, anagram-face.

Mammy. That was my mother. She's dead, like Perfection, but it never makes any difference, does it?

Daddy. That was my father. He was misplaced. We didn't find him for so long. His misplacement didn't make any difference, either. It's funny what doesn't. Your everyday grumbles and the slant words of dictators: they seem to infect every corner of your life, don't they? But why? I will tell you of terrible deaths and high tides that took centuries and mermaids that could walk and love like no other. *That* is the sort of thing that should make a difference, but we'll see.

I was saying:

Bronwen Llewhellin. My grandmother. She's dead, but extremely active and her teeth go clackety-clack and she won't have them fixed because it's vanity.

Eleri No-name. That second bit is a mystery waiting for you to solve. She was my great-grandmother, also dead, but never greater.

Miss Davies. Now she was a rich elderly lady, the crabbed keeper of Clandestine House on the pretty estuary I will bring alive for you. She looked after me, in her own way. Paid for things I needed. Always her house changed and the pictures in her frames were never of people she knew, but always new, creeping along the wall.

Seren. A beauty. She was Miss Davies's adopted daughter. A sour, suffering beauty.

Rhys. He was a good man. I didn't prize him as I should have done. He was my brother in law, husband to Perfection. She treated him like a child, lectured and harangued. But he cared for her well and he painted and he made.

Muffled Myfanwy Llewhellin was my aunt. Her voice stopped when she lost her son, Lewis, the Younger. Sometimes it came out in a hoarse whisper, but always her place in the world was minute. She looked out across The Sound, but never said what she saw out there. But I managed to help her change things—*oh yes*. And she did well to get a job with the Dead Dears and Evans, who loved them so.

Philip Llewhellin. Now, he was my uncle, that is, Myfanwy's husband, and dead by hanging. Not a character as such but I honour the dead, so there you are, see.

Lewis (the Younger) Llewhellin, Myfanwy's son, dead by shooting over the shuffle-board. As I said before, I am honouring him here and in the poem I see you put at the very beginning, which was kind of you, girl.

Lewis (the First) Llewhellin. He was a school teacher, stern but we loved him. He had been found deceased, in a bed of violets, with a half smile on his face. Circumstances suspicious.

Derian Llewhellin. A mysterious, wild man and supposed criminal. He appeared in a sea cave.

Nerys and Dilys. Two lovely mermaids; they were friends to me. They taught me so much about the beauties of the body and the spirit. Don't be shy when I describe them, promise? And, you know, mermaids have their own special history and stories and sometimes they creep across the land.

Evans the Bodies. Undertaker. I was apprenticed to him. Learned a fine trade of the Dead Dears. He was happier with the waxy bodies than any body he'd known in much life. I think they understood him better. And Myfanwy came into his life, you know. I helped her to, as I always seek to help: with a story.

Gwyneth. She came to help Perfection and Rhys at my childhood home. Perfection chided her and was jealous because she had a certain beauty and Rhys looked at her from the corner of his eye and smiled. I saw him and he knew that I'd seen.

Williams, a lawyer. A rich thing of the darkness. A Welshman who became an Englishman, for shame.

Ned Owens. My friend in Bath, a coastal who went posh.

Roland Griffiths. A cruel but manly landowner; courted Seren. I hated him, And I had reason.

Oh, Catherine. Are you listening carefully and can you remember them all? I know there is much there, but you asked for a story and here is a story of one of my lives. The story of how I got my name and travelled, travelled, travelled. And I have written the names down for you, look, see. You can refer back, if you need. There is a whole world in what I have noted.

But Almost, how did you know I would want a story? You prepared your characters ahead for me. And yet... this story seems familiar to me.

This is why I came. Why I always come. And the story is always true and familiar. Nothing is new, girl. There are just things as yet unseen and links unmade.

I am ready for the story now, Almost.

And so Almost began and he was on fire with beauty and delight and with a sadness that was victorious.

3

Christmas eve at the sea cave

That day, I sat under the slowly darkening sky and I thought that no-one knew where I spent my stolen afternoons. I was dragged up, not brought up; when scrubbed or slapped, I would slip out here to the wilds by the sea and contemplate what lay there.

What did?

First there was the old graveyard; then there was the strange old boat; beyond that was the wide, wide sea, which siren-called me with peculiar voices that somehow I had always known. I've been lonely. I've got a stupid name, for a start—and it tends to put people off: *Almost*. It must have been my mother's little joke. Maybe she gave it to me so that I would reach for the stars and transcend the limits of the name, but I suspect it was because she wanted to keep me down there: a not quite, just about, more or less kind of kid. And that's what I was.

Until that day, when the darkness fell slowly and I stayed out late.

It was Christmas eve and inside homes the trees sparkled with a spiteful beauty; I could see them on the headland, winking at me as the sea whipped. I kept walking, just picking up shells as I went and filling my pockets. On the beach, the moored jellyfish trembled and I could see spits of tar and dead horseshoe crabs; sometimes a sea potato thrust up—sometimes intact: the most beautiful thing you ever saw and like a miniature moon, with a roughened velvet coat and tidy little seams. *Echinocardium*. But it was hard to cradle one in your hand and keep it safe. I walked on and on until I met the sea cave. I shouldn't have been out this late, the darkness dropping so heavily and the tide coming in fast, too fast and for too long, but I loved the cave and its dark, salty rocks, its ancient fissures and rivulets; its dank, familiar smell that said, 'Stay here Almost: I will keep you afloat and no-one will be able to find you.'

But I thought I heard something on the breeze and it said, 'Help me!'

Did I hear it? No surely it was imagined, so I climbed the cliff path and went to visit all my dead friends and relatives at Capel Dewi, our headland church.

I had been to call on Philip Llewhellin, who hanged himself, and Philip's brother, the old schoolmaster, Lewis The First Llewhellin, who was found expired, mysterious but happy, in a mound of violets, from which vantage point he had often been seen observing tankers headed in and out of Milford Haven; I saw from a distance that, visiting the old churchyard with a Christmas wreath, there was Muffled Myfanwy Llewhellin, so small and pretty and, for epochs, unable to say a word while she brewed tea, knitted for the jumble or did cakes to raise money for the lifeboat. She had a voice once, but it had got stifled when her son, Lewis the Younger, had killed himself, like his father, over what no-one knew. She didn't speak for years and when, eventually, she did, startling the women in the post office when she she asked for a book of second class stamps, it was quiet and as if she were speaking through a heavy knitted scarf and then at a whisper and then she was always *Muffled Myfanwy who lived on the hill and who had found her dead husband hanging in the shed above his hoes and rakes and who had lost her son to a gun across the shuffle-board in The Sloop.*

Muffled Myfanwy had once stood for hours, like her husband Philip, looking out across the bay. Sometimes, she was gazing from the little lifeboat station at St Justinian across the Sound to Ramsey Island; she would cock her ear to something, but what it was she could hear, no-one could say. And why she bought stamps, no-one ever knew since they never saw her writing or posting. *Secrets, secrets.* Once, I took her a shell from the beach, thinking that she lived too sad for flowers. One time, when I was younger, I took her a book of stamps, too, thinking that she liked those. Each time I saw her, I wanted to make her better and release the muffled voice.

So that was the others. Then there was my grandmother

and Nanny, or great grandmother, Eleri and Bronwen. United in death, as in life, but probably not in Heaven yet because they still had too much meddling to do on earth. Eleri birthed handfuls, roomfuls of children; all dispersed; Bronwen managed them, smoking her pipe and spitting at strangers; peeling potatoes and killing pigs, or at least that was how I remember her. I adored Bronwen and Eleri but didn't know how or why they had died, other than that their ends had been not far apart and, hopefully, demise had been preceded by a satisfying look at the little white lady in the corner of the room, a sort of Welsh Virgin Mary, with rolled up sleeves that Nanny began to see as she became more old and frail. The Blessed Virgin smoked a pipe too because it was stressful being the mother of Jesus, what with all the intercessions and all. And she was apparently a roarer with the swearing, like.

And then there was Mammy. That was the most difficult. Daddy was misplaced. Some said he had run off with a Tenby schoolmistress or a rich spinster, but I hadn't known what had happened to him and anyway, he had always been a bit shadowy, a bit short on substance, so that when he was there, he was hardly there at all. But Mammy continued. On flame and beautiful. Oh, she was *beautiful*. I never wanted to go home because I could hardly bear to look at her. Men courted her, strange and good, but she sent them off. She was the finest woman, but she was oh so cruel. I had always wanted a proper name, but she hadn't given me one. Instead I got 'Almost' and she told me that one day I would understand my name. I was so little when I lost them, but then my memory is engraved and expansive; I record and remember everything, don't I? But Mammy: that day, as the darkness fell still more, I hated her so much for the name. The other children laughed at my strangeness and, I think, at how separate I was from them. It wasn't fair. I had shells for her, but when I went to lay them down, I felt a wash of rage and I hurled them over the lych-gate and back toward the cliff.

Why, Mammy?

I didn't know why she died, only that she had. Or Bronwen, clackety-clack, or Eleri. Where did they all go? When I'd asked, people changed the subject. Because I was still so young, I lived with my older sister, whose name, gratingly, incongruously, was Perfection, as I told, but came also under the care of the crabbed elderly lady, Miss Davies, who lived out on the Cleddau Estuary and whom I loved with a passion. Perfection was almost as nasty (so I, boy, thought) as my mother and tonight I could be up for a rattling and shaming, dirty little boy. And suddenly, with these thoughts, I was angry and violent, and yet as muffled up as Myfanwy, so with the last shreds of day, I turned on my heel and ran for the purple beach. There was time to rail and scream it out in the sea cave before it was too dark and the tide was still low enough.

I was breathless from my scramble down the cliff and my pelt for the cave. I leaned against its walls and closed my eyes, willing something bigger than us all and more kind to lift me up and put me somewhere else, but only taking my beautiful sea cave with us.

Then came a man.

He was filthy, brutal-looking and ragged and he was running towards me at top speed, the water hurling itself against his filthy clothes and gnarled legs, as if to stop him getting to me. But the eyes of the man pleaded; dark pools, speaking to me. I was scared, but I had to help him.

'Help me boy. Don't be scared. I won't hurt you.'

He was beside me.

How could I help?

'The men are coming for me and I am starving and need some clean clothes, food and a place to hide.'

'Are you a criminal?' I asked. I was shaking, but somehow I knew that he would not hurt me.

'Yes, they say I am. They say I killed a man.'

This made me cry.

'Don't be frightened. I didn't kill him. I found him. My friend. It was old Llewhellin, the schoolmaster. Did you know him? Lived on the headland in the little white bungalow. An old man, always as old as the hills.'

'He was my uncle.'

'Oh boy, I am sorry. He was a good man. I went to ask for his help. I found him out there, face down in a bed of violets, bruised and flower-stained. He was half smiling. I thought he had fallen. I turned him and he was cold, half-smiling, and dead, boy. But I didn't kill him. They say I did and that I took his money from the mattress, but it was not me, *not:* I swear to you.'

The man had tears in his eyes. I believed him. His dark eyes told me he was an honest man, fallen on tragedy and felled further by the brutal lies of this very part of Wales.

'Will you help me? There is no-one else. I went to Our Lady out at St Non's, but she was too busy with the other sinners, she said.'

'I will.'

'I need, boy, clean clothes and some food. Some shoes. Can you do this? Can you get me just a little money so I can catch the train and the ferry and get away from here, although I don't know yet where I should go.'

'But… aren't you on the run from the law? They think you are a murderer.'

'We are all on the run from something, boy.'

This made sense to me.

'I will help. But what is your name?'

'Derian Llewhellin.'

'Llewhellin—with that funny spelling, like mine, the bad 'h' that Miss Jenkins said was an English corruption of proper Welsh and an insult to Prince Llewelyn—or the proper one?'

'Oh boy, I have an 'h' like you. We are both scoundrels.'

'Are you family to me then?'

'No, but we will, I think, be linked.' The man's dark eyes glittered. 'Philip that hanged himself and Lewis the First and Lewis the Younger, poor lad, were kin, of kind, to me. I… watched over them, I like to think.'

'Then it is as if you are family to me!'

Now the man had tears in his eyes: 'They do not talk about

me here. I am a long story to tell; a bad story. They wish me hanged too. Some think I am hanged already.'

A strange thing to say: 'But I like stories, good and bad. I long to hear the story of your life.'

'One day, boy, perhaps, is it; when time is different and the world is away. Yes, maybe. But...what is your name?'

'Do not laugh. It is Almost.'

The man looked at me intently: 'That is a better name than *Never* or *Cannot* or *There*.'

Again, this made sense.

There is no there, *there*.

I turned. Food shoes, clothes. A little money.

'You cannot stay here in your wet clothes. Come with me and I will hide you in Rhys's workshop tonight. You will drown in the sea cave or catch your death of cold. And you know, there are creatures and voices here that may not be so kind to you. Let's wait for more darkness to fall and then we will go.'

So the sea talked and the crab shells and the jellyfish were beached and I heard the auger shells whisper on the sand and I remembered a poem that my sister Perfection once taught me; it was about the fine conical shells, rosy pink and amaranth and a little copper, with their rounded layers and sharp points and their telling mystery. Perfection was cruel, but still, she had an eye for beauty. And an auger: a sign or premonition of something—*that* had a tinge of excitement to it. And so I looked at the natural world as though it were a series of metaphors for the life hereafter.

But then sometimes I would tingle in case the auger might be of some rough beast, slouching preternaturally towards St David's Head. Still, I remembered and even composed poems that sounded… *old*, to make sense of this rough world with its expectation, and all; its feeling that the tide world I saw was communicating something else to me in its argot: 'Listen, boy: this is not all, but here is all.' Yes, I composed; printed the poems on my memory, shabby bard-boy, because if I wrote them Perfection might find them and toss them out with the peelings: 'What good are those for you or to me!' She had an eye for beauty but a cruel hand with the written record. So,

The Auger shell, unbroken, in the palm,
still yet, such tenor of this hour upon this tide,
I wait at The Haven, looking out to sea:
you do not come. I nurse the shell,
its whorls and tidy chambers tell
of secrets and of things I cannot know;
the grains of sand, or filament of carapace
swept up inside its little maze,
its rooms, its tidy cap, once came from elsewhere,
elsewhere on this tide, I'll never know. And you,
I wait for, mute, looking out to sea. I hear you laugh
and cannot say from where it came, as seabirds circle low.
I throw the shell where anemone and spider crab
have made their home—more life reclaims it now,
as your laugh is lost to me, in warm thrift and gorse
and the tenor of this hour upon the tide.

And I thought about whether this was an important moment, while we waited for the darkness to further settle. The man touched my arm with a ragged hand and I felt… I felt a kind of electricity; a blurring of my edges, my form. I was not sure of my dimensions, my time or place. And then back again I was, on the cold sand. And everything was different. I just did not know how yet.

I decided it was a moment on which a life turned. I knew it was.

It was Christmas eve and inside the trees sparkled with a spiteful beauty; I could see them on the headland, winking at me as the sea whipped. *Climb, Almost.*

4

Perfection, Charity and Clandestine

Sometimes our freedom is not where we expect it, but positioned somewhere between rock and rock. As a boy, when I was so sad, I ran out a long long way in the darkness. Even then, the white and red of the old lighthouse in the cleft cliffs at St Justinian were numinous, attracting midday at midnight if the moon caught right. I remembered, then, being out on the boats, heading for The Bitches, which is what we call the little rushes of current, minuscule but voluble waterfalls between the mainland and the island, and I would sense, then too, freedom come up from soft seabed and feel the clench of my girls' arms: Dilys and Nerys, my mermaid girls.

You're wondering whether mermaids are real? *Of course.* And they are for all time and all pleasure. I had never not known them and what I will tell you later on may shock a little. A deep and capable pleasure. For that I know you will wait. So I will go on.

The cleft cliff, the boats out, the arms of the girls and freedom between rock and rock, so, committed to memory,

St Justinian at dawn; the boat,
its clenched hull scowling,
as braced against the swell,
collected errant figures—all
adrift, so lost on land, and sad.
We reached out, emptied souls,
to Ramsey Sound; the island
siren-called us, brought us home
to sea: to stay afloat a while
and find our shipwrecked selves.

It wasn't in the landing of our craft,
against the crashing deck of shore,
but somewhere in between the rock
and rock, that melancholy came to rest—
and tumbled down through navy depths
and we were free, unbroken: still.

But on Christmas eve, under cover of kind dark and encouraged by the love of my girls far out at sea, Derian and I sloshed through the rising tide and back across the long beach as the gulls called and swooped. He didn't say much now and I noticed that his breaths sometimes came in sharp jags; here and there a little wheeze.

'Far, boy?'

Back across the long beach, feeling the wet sand clog our boots, I felt a strange surge of happiness wrapped up with danger. Danger because I now knew he was thought to be a bad man, and because I knew I would be in great trouble when we reached Charity House and Perfection, whose eyes would be burning across the dark headland, boring a channel to Ireland, almost, (almost—I laughed when I thought about how I'd used the word) and ready and lusty to be violent to me. She kept an old hairbrush just for that purpose and called it *Nabob*; she'd got the name from my father's copy of *Hobson Jobson's Anglo-Indian Dictionary* (although I suspect Perfection would have struggled to find India on a map or tell you what the English had all to do there and God man, for it had nothing to do with our Wales). And happiness, oh yes: because I felt different. The blurring of the edges, as I told you, begun when the ragged man brushed my arm.

Climbing the shingle, scuffing along the sea lane and then up over the little coast road toward home, Derian dragged behind me.

'Come on, almost there!' (I'd done it again.)

'Are we *there* or *nearly* or *more or less*, Almost?' I laughed. Derian was ragged, but not beaten yet. And so, through the wrought iron gate with the legend *Charity House* twirled within its struts—and then time to keep low and still.

'There, Derian. The low white building at back. Run to it, close to the ground. I'll keep watch.' He did as I asked. And just in time.

'Where have you been you thankless little whelp?' boomed my sister.

'Looking for whelp-whelks.' She would thrash me whatever I said. She began by cuffing me with the butt of her torch. Inside, Nabob the brush must have been bridling, ready for it.

'Inside now. How dare you run out on Christmas eve!'

Boom.

Slap.

'If you think hitting you with Nabob is the worst I can do!'

Perfection meant well, in her own way. Because our father was misplaced somewhere and mother was dead (although still exerting an influence, it seemed), she had taken charge and bullishly so. Perfection was not a pretty woman, but she was a worker. She and Rhys toiled away in the shop, for long, long hours; everyone loved him and most people disliked her for her temper. After hours, Rhys would retreat to paint or make things in the workshop. Once sketches of the beach; St Govan's, the chapel in the cleft rock, the walk down to Barafundle and an otter he'd watched at play in the Bosherston Lily Ponds as he walked through the Stackpole Estate to Broad Haven South and its beautiful spit of beach. Pembroke Castle; ruins of old farmhouses; Pentre Ifan on the Preselis from where, as we all learned in school, they took the blue-stones for Stonehenge.

'Though why anyone would want to leave Pembrokeshire and why they didn't just build it there, with a proper view, I don't know,' said our class teacher.

In the garden, Rhys, her husband, my brother in law, built pebble sculptures, which Perfection swiped at with the mower and sometimes he created sunset scenes of of our yellow beaches with oil pastels and I never saw him happier, this gentle man, as he massaged the colours into one another and they spread up his arms and roundly into my heart, forever. He wanted and deserved more. He wanted a woman for whom he was not lackey and butt of jokes and who did not perceive him as weak. *He* was perfection; she was sin, though I doubt really it was that simple. Truly though, Perfection was dim and rough and Rhys was delicate and artistic, though never a success in school and his reading was patchy. I always wished I could share them with him: the books. Perfection never hit him with Nabob, but her acid tongue lashed and he never stood up to her; he let her humiliate and mock him. Once, when she pushed him, he let her; once, when she hit him with the flat of her hand, I thought, for a second, he would retaliate. But he didn't. Though I, outraged child, jumped on her back and pulled her hair and cried, 'Don't hurt him.'

Throwing me off, I knew Nabob was coming and that Rhys would visit me later and tell me stories and mop my tears and say, 'You and I, Almost, have never been a success with women. Mammy; Perfection; it's all the same. But we do our best and must be gentle—gentle men.' And then I would sleep and dream of the other times and the mermaids and strange creatures in the sea cave, after dark.

Now, Perfection went to cook my Christmas eve supper,

like a curse, and I could slip out with bread and cheese and some apples for my new convict friend-uncle. And, from the laundry drying by the fire, I took a heavy winter work shirt of Rhys's and trousers and socks and an old coat from the under-stairs cupboard and a towel and did what I had promised to do. And I took some money from Perfection's housekeeping jar and now Nabob would be fierce in its punishment and for the lies I would openly tell on Christmas morning.

'Thank you boy. You are a good boy. Merry Christmas to you.'

That night, I had no stocking as punishment and the Christmas tree twinkled sarcastically. I was Almost again. Couldn't tell a lie. Couldn't even run away with my new-found friend-uncle. But I was glad to help him. In the dark of Christmas morning, I brought him bread and a mug of cocoa and more apples and a slab of Christmas supper ham and when I went back to cover any traces, he was gone. To something better, I hoped. I felt we would meet again.

So Christmas morning saw me with coins and nuts and clementines and five pounds secretly pushed to me by Rhys and then I was told we had been sent for to visit Clandestine House, up the Cleddau Estuary, to have our Christmas day with Miss Davies, the nasty, dusty old spinster whom I loved and who set me right for books and things I needed for school and for growing up because when Mammy died and Daddy was misplaced, so was the family's money and Miss Davies had a heart, dusty as it was. And then there was Seren, her sniping beautiful adopted daughter, whom I loved more than life itself. *Seren*, for *star*. *Seren ar gyfer seren* in my imperfect Welsh from behind the Landsker line.

Clandestine House might, in other times, have been beautiful. Seen from a distance, perhaps it still was. A fine Georgian building, with an orchard behind, *the haggard* as Miss Davies called it, and flower borders and rockeries in front, all with an insolent beauty. It looked out across the little harbour and stood adjacent to the pretty Clandestine Arms, the village pub. You could hear the calls of the sea birds, smell the salty mud and listen to the cree of the curlews across the water. It was a changing land, with a whirling navy sky above it and centuries of other people's histories wrapped up in its dark heart. Yes—dark. The house was darkness visible. Miss Davies, treated cruelly other than with riches by her parents, mocked by her horrid brother and let down in love by her fiancé, had curled in upon herself. He dress was navy or black, seldom changed, her eyes were deep aphotic pools and her powdery skin pulled back tightly over once-lovely cheekbones.

The room was crepuscular, but there was to be a feast, with tapers.

'Help me, Almost.' And as I heard it I remembered the call for help out by my sea cave on the long beach. I wondered of Derian and felt, again, the tremor of electricity, so it seemed, down my arm with his touch. Things were swimming; happening.

I wandered in the strange house where books, many of which I read, were legion. In her library there was a book, spine open, on the floor. It was Shakespeare's *Pericles.* When I picked it up, my eye was drawn to the lines 'You shall prevail, were it to woo my daughter, for it seems you have been noble towards her.' The beloved child of the King Pericles, Marina, presumed lost at sea, breaks a heart, is found and loved. I replaced the book on a shelf and closed a window strangely ajar in this fusty Christmas house. I touched a salt breeze and shivered.

Now, Miss Davies moved creakily towards the kitchen and I felt her claw-fingers stroke my back. She was hardened and suffering, but she felt love for me, despite her hatred for the world. And then there was Seren, bringing the dishes and the salvers and the goose and the roasted apples and the potatoes and bread sauce and gravy and red cabbage and glasses of good things and Christmas cake and the brandy-spiked pudding with its coin and the matches and the cream and the silverware and I loved her and I loved her and I loved her and I knew I would never ever see that returned, though she would tease me and give me a sense of being hers, almost. She, too, was unhappy but wanted to break my heart because her own world had been shattered and was ever constricting further, in the black and navy night world of Clandestine House and the quay.

The food and its salvers were luxurious but the table was dusty; above the table, dark penumbrous strands of cobweb hung from the chandeliers, a joke of golden strands. The furniture had been moved again, leaving, where floor and wall were now exposed, dim whorls of dust. And

Seren—star—served dinner and Miss Davies picked at it all, like a timid or sated bird—and Perfection made stilted conversation while the eyes of the other females burned in unseen scorn.

In my head, I wrote Miss Davies a poem, because that is what I did to take my mind off Seren. And at Clandestine House and at the quay, I had a sense of being surrounded by a living, breathing creature. Not the people; nothing animal—but in the house, itself. It was alive. I thought that Miss Davies constantly moved the furniture, but I was not sure. Wherever you went at Clandestine, you were not alone. The photographs changed and were of no-one I knew; the walls were warm, without the benefit of heating: something was happening here. And I felt, at the quay, that something was happening in the world beyond. That the curlews screamed and harangued the foolish people that came that way; that moss and weed grew fast and that the kelp was thrown up too far and too thickly; the pink thrift too vigorous. I felt it, too, on the long beach near our house, the night I met Derian. There were things that were alive—or more than alive; a preternatural world, but whether wholly good or bad I could not, as yet, translate. And the things that were long dead walked with as much colour and vehemence as the present living. I thought I saw a hunger burn in the eyes of old Miss Davies and Seren; and I thought I felt a hunger in the land around me. And I thought the house had needs too—and that all three communed in some way in a dull echo and saw it through a yellow look from out the corner of my eye. And trying not to look at Seren, radiant in her scorn, and eating my wonderful meal on a dusty table under a cobweb-trimmed gilt chandelier, I made a poem, imprinted on memory, of course.

Around here, the trees suck air and, at night,
when the last shriek of the plump and pretty-breasted curlew
is drawn from its throat, and when the strand-line treasure
is dulled and shredded against the rock, even in fair weather,
well then: that is the time that the houses take their fill.
Miss Davies, is it true? Oh yes. Around here, when the moss
spawns bad, it creeps across your foot if you slowly move,
to be sure to move quite fast, when the twilight stalks,
then that is the time that the houses take their fill.
Miss Davies, is it true? Oh yes. When the jewel sky
and the lapping wing have beat their very blood
into the hour, take heed; the tidiest stones
we built home with, will stretch up so to bark and gulp
at silly men, while *we* shall know what is to come,
as groaning, crafted stone leans in
to kiss a sleeping face and staunch, in wild, oh wild, rebellion,
dear,
the men that wrest it proudly from the ground.

And I was scared, then. And I hoped that Derian was clear of this strange world where all, as I thought, he had done was find his dead friend in a mound of violets and find himself a convicted man. And I went out, as they talked and played their cards without any joy, and I stood on the edge of the quay as the tide was coming in and I called for my friends. I knew they would not let me down. You *know* I was never like other boys, my tender story-listening friend, I have you now, and I have others with lives to change and for whom I must tell a story, but back then it was Dilys and Nerys. They were grown women, but they were of the sea. You don't believe in mermaids? Did you ever read *The Wizard of Oz*? Now, its author knew all about mermaids and when his storyteller went out on the boats, she began to understand that there was a whole world of them and they were so very fine: I can remember this part of the story and I thought of it as I waited for my girls:

...the mermaids were clothed, too, and their exquisite gowns were the loveliest thing the little girl had ever beheld. They seemed made of a material that was like sheeny silk, cut low in the neck and with wide, flowing sleeves that seldom covered the shapely, white arms of her new friends. The gowns had trains that floated far behind the mermaids as they swam, but were so fleecy and transparent that the sparkle of their scales might be seen reaching back of their waists, where the human form ended and the fish part began.

I felt hot, *hot*, when I said that aloud. Do you feel it too?

And do you know that, round these parts, it is said—and oh, it is true—that the sea fairies wear strings of splendid pearls twined around their throats, while more pearls are sewn upon their gowns for trimmings. Their beautiful hair is not trimmed up, but left floating around them in clouds.

I have seen this at high and low tide, slick on the water. Inviting.

And I called them, Nerys and Dilys, as I knew I could, with a low whistle and they came to me, mothering me and caressing me and I told them about my meeting in the sea cave and about Perfection's anger; then I told them about the house and they said it was not as strange as sea-world, but it was not as beautiful because of its sadness. And they whispered to me, Nerys and Dilys—I tried to look away, from their milky breasts and their pitch-dark eyes and the delicate purpling around their eyes the colour of kelp at high tide under the happiest rainbow, but I could not. Their sensuality was innocent, not brazen and they stroked my arms and reassured me that I had the powers to change my course, that they had sensed something begun with the wild ragged man (they knew? Of course, for the sea talks). And they said that Seren and Miss Davies were in a world beyond sad and that Miss Davies had been let down by the love of her life and scorned by her whole family, so she made her world anew and created its own peculiar untruth; a tissue of lies—the people in the photographs were not known to her; she cut pieces from old papers and put them in frames and imagined they were her family and her story; frequently she lugged the heavy furniture from room to room and made the house new. But each time, the thoughts came back and she found that her thought, substantial, animated the rooms and took no note of the material change she had made.

And here is more about my girls and their world. Wait:

yes, I have it all now, from an old, old book, committed to memory over a long time. So,

Beneath the depths of the ocean, according to these stories, an atmosphere exists adapted to the respiratory organs of certain beings, resembling, in form, the human race, possessed of surpassing beauty, of limited supernatural powers, and liable to the incident of death. They dwell in a wide territory of the globe, far below the region of fishes, over which the sea, like the cloudy canopy of our sky, loftily rolls, and they possess habitations constructed of the pearl and coral productions of the ocean.

Hot, hot again!

And, oh: isn't that a fine thing?

And there is this. Remember, girl. Remember. For when they come on land, they are curious to watch and understand the workings of the human race, or rather the land folk, and they take off their sea dress and put on a land garb. And off they shimmy to examine us; our clay foot folly. Sometimes, because they are kind and loyal and because they possess an understanding of the depths, of depths of feeling, they come too. When I have been mad, beaten, alone, full of frosty demons or lusts, they came for me. Sometimes to take me back into the sea.

Your mermaid girls are so adaptable, but they are vulnerable too. They can come on land as elk or mouse, or woman, man, some binary confection, but each merman or merwoman possesses yet one skin, one sea garb, enabling the individual to ascend the seas, and if, in our land abode, that garb be lost, the hapless being must unavoidably become an inhabitant of the earth.

Now that is interesting, Almost.

Interesting? Ha. It is a green miracle. But remember that last detail, reader; friend: if the garb be lost, the hapless being must unavoidably become an inhabitant of the earth and this is terrible suffering for a sea creature. Yes, remember that detail.

Why, Almost?

Shh. I was coming to that. At some point. So, my sea girls have always swum to me when I needed them and they know about the human world because, as this old book tells you, they explore the landways in animal form and they wait and listen. As a doe, Nerys looked through the windows of Clandestine House and watched Miss Davies try to make her nest anew, wresting the photos from the paper and crying as she did it. Sometime, Dilys sat as a wren on the windowsill of the house and heard what Miss Davies said to Seren.

'Break their hearts, girl. The world is too much with us, all men are cads, there is filth under the wrack and the green sea is no place to sail away on. Make yourself a carapace of bitterness, Seren. Make yourself a cruel, lovely, burning star. Break their hearts.'

And Seren would cry, but she would nod assent and so sing a poem or song of the deep sea, printed on memory, of course, in case Miss Davies tossed out its scrawled libretto with today's photographs and life history: 'Ohhhhh' she howled to the sea and then,

Oh never fill your heart with trawlermen
my Nanny told, then told: You want
a man with both feet on the ground—
a man with roughened nails, from
dirt and labour on the land,
not brined and drenched through by the sea.
But Nanny never knew the sound
of oilskin slipped on clover bank;
of danger in the stolen hull,
of silver, limned above your head,
while thwart hands toiled through the night,
and washed me up and brought me home.
I wouldn't learn.
I dreamed of pearls, full fathom five;
I sang of gales, the tang of salt,
the storied depths of sea and sea—
limb-frozen journeys, far from home
with yellow light on midnight crests.
But Nanny told, then told, You want
a man with bone-dry shoes, inland;
your sailors leave you high and dry,
they catch and throw and pack in ice
the keenest heart that you can toss.
But Nanny never knew the song
of siren journeys way out there,
of labour stoked by heat and loss—
she didn't feel the azure pull,
the mermaid kiss, the tongues that spoke;

she died a desiccated death, in clod
that choked, while primrose mocked.
Still, far offshore, I rocked and bobbed:
we drew the finest catch that day.

5

Dressing the Dead Dears

Here is a fragment of memory. Sunday afternoons of grave dressing, far and wide. Of a strained scant picnic amongst the stones, while the sea dragged in from Broad Haven, below, a down heaven of sorts, beyond the blackberry hedge. This is the bit before we left for Walton, Talbenny, Neyland to buff up the Llewhellins and those poor souls, otherwise, who lay forgotten. I wondered if they preferred it that way but didn't dare say or risk the first years of Nabob or a lash from Mammy, Eleri or Bronwen, dead or alive. It went like this, the chat before we left home, with kit for the deceased:

Boy, get the grave bag from by the back door!
I'm doing it now, in a minute!
But have you got there the water in the milk bottle,
the scrubber and the cloth and the scissors,
they're rusty but will do to trim?

Yes, yes, I see them now.
But have you got them, have you? We mustn't forget
and mustn't leave the bag at home and mustn't take it
to the graves half-full: is it done now, is it all and are you sure?
The westerlies and the tongues of salt are cruel to our dead
and all their stones.
Yes, I am sure.
The bag was bundled and the car was roared and the dead
were glad
of a well-kept stone and the brambles trimmed and no-one
cursed,
like they did, all did, in life, and the door was keyed and the
grave bag was refilled
and sat just as it should, and the life was endless not altered,
even in this loud new world.

There now, let me tell you about a fine friend and teacher. Perhaps, soon, you will meet him and he will care for you. He cared for *them* in the loud new world, kept things old but, you see, he was also in want. He loved until his heart burst. I loved this man and I felt… I was different now. You remember how I told you that my edges blurred that Christmas Eve at the sea cave with the convict Derian Llewhellin? He touched my arm and I felt, I felt, that I could do more and that if I used my voice proper-like, well it could move those who were stifled or silent with sadness to speak again; to voice poetry. It's not that I was special…

Ah. *But Almost, you are.* Is that what your eyes are telling me, girl?

I tell back, *Oh… oh, land girl..I am not.* What gifts I have were given to me; I did not earn them! But as I was saying, I had a sense that I could prompt the unwillingly quiet person to sing and, as you know, I think now that a story can shift a continent or, at the very least, pull you, my darling, from your sad overshadowed world to the green sea of all time. So, let me acquaint you with my friend; a favourite tale, this, and more than one story in it. The first is for Evans, fine lad; the second about how you may find love in the desert. I see you look perplexed. Let me tell this.

Evans the Bodies loved his Dead Dears. He had established a thriving business in the low white farm buildings out the back of a farm on the coast road. In the past, this had been owned by a rather careless and drunken farmer with an insecure barn so that, from time, those who arrived for Evans's attention—silently, so silently—might have met with a stray cow crossing the yard or traversed cow pats, so hardly the most respectful of endings, or beginnings, as Evans saw it, since he was fonder of the dead than the living and saw things backwards through his better eye. Nowadays, though, the yard was gravelled, the whitewash immaculate, the cows tidily restrained and a new farmer in residence. This man was laughed at by the locals as a hobby farmer. A man with an antique shop in Tenby who got people in to do the hard work and exhibited his cheese to great applause, although he had not really made it himself and even his dairy herd looked askance, it was said on the coast road, because your dairy cow knew an amateur when it saw one and mocked in its cow-grunt while you flaunted your wares in front of the Aga. Still, at least our dead weren't shit-mired before they were interred.

So there, in his low white buildings, worked Evans. And I went to work with him when I was older, into my teenage years; I was a poor schoolboy, so they farmed me out on an apprenticeship as soon as they could. Technically, I should have been eighteen to be allowed to handle the dead, but we hid from the rules, I looked big and talked confidently and bluffed expertly and then Evans—at least to begin with—kept me away from the worst, most gruesome cases. He needn't have done, for I saw no fear in temporal things and the sad features of a face rearranged; I saw them as the anagram of thereafter. The day when Derian brushed my arm and the edges were... indefinite, now that is important to our story: to what is life; what is death; what is in between and round about. But as I was saying, I worked with him, learned from the master and saw how he attended carefully to his craft. He had it all planned meticulously and liked to recite the rules of his job to himself and declaim thus to the world, should it be listening. Yet the best of the words were not really for me, but for the woman he had loved his whole life and whose own life and voice had been taken by the abruptly dead of her own.

For with him worked Muffled Myfanwy.

I mentioned her, to you, in my list of characters. She went muffled after Philip Llewhellin hanged himself in the shed and then her son, Lewis the Younger, remember? Evans was in love with this quiet sad lady and together they worked with the corpses, a delicate ballet, with tubes and brushes and buckets and pipes and the love of the dead that is known best to those sad with the living, or those born, or otherwise, with their feet half in the next world. He had dressed and buried her husband and son and allowed himself only to breathe, 'You should not have'. He had placed, under the hands of her brother in law, the schoolmaster, found in a mound of violets, a tiny bunch of the blooms with a sprig of rosemary: love, faithfulness and remembrance. And I watched Evans and Myfanwy in the twilight shadows, Always I was there. Because he was lonely, even with his Dead Dears and she was sad and her voice was stilled and I wanted to give her flight and for her to sing and cast off her own dead. And then there was the very intimacy of it: he had washed and nursed her lost son and sent him lovingly to his resting place; he had done the same for her lost husband and even though the woman he loved was married to the man and the man had made her suffer and his son had made her suffer, he nursed them and prepared them in death and felt their deep sadness, though he did allow himself to whisper chastisements, as I said, but also, 'I will take care of her now' to both men. And when Llewhellin the schoolmaster was found in his mound of violets, he took care to place his poetry book under the hands and, within it, though no-one knew, he had pressed those violets from the mound because of how much their musky sweetness had been adored.

Now, because Evans the Bodies so loved his muffled

company, he would narrate what he was doing, like a child before it learns that it does not have to describe itself in the third or fourth person. Thus, 'Now Myfanwy, as you know the first step in the embalming process of our Dead Dears is a surgical one, in which bodily fluids are removed with our special pipes and tubes and are then replaced with formaldehyde-based chemical solutions. The second step, mind Myfanwy and as you know, Myfanwy, is cosmetic, in which the body is prepared for viewing by styling the Dead Dears' hair, applying some make-up, and setting the facial features so they don't frighten their loved ones, all ghastly like. Whatever end they had, Myfanwy, we must make them look well and tidy. Mrs Morgan of the tractor accident will take a bit of work, mind, so you'll have to be cunning with the makeup and the brush, a bit of padding and a dress that they bought in the posh shop in Newcastle Emlyn.'

Between them, Evans and Myfanwy lifted the dead man onto the table and Evans began gently sloshing from his vat of disinfectant and washed the body of Jones The Angry from Begelly. He hadn't been a good man; he was a mean old man, but he was lonely and hurt by the world and Evans knew this and when he washed it was like a baptism. As he went, he signed the cross when he remembered and felt he should, but sometimes he went round and round like he was doodling spirals—or sometimes shooting stars; sometimes a maze.

'There we are now, Myfanwy. Rub Mr Jones's feet. Ah now, look at the skill you do that with. I will massage and manipulate—he's a stiff one, this Dead Dear and his muscles are hard with the rigor, so we'll have to loosen him or he'll look like a board and won't be well for the funeral and he'll startle the congregation. I had one once that sat up. Now, the neighbours say we should shave him but I think he suits a bit of beard, don't you Myfanwy? A new look for the old boy! There we are, isn't it? He's more relaxed already. I do think it's the way you do their feet, Myfanwy. It is your rare gift, Myfanwy.'

It was a strange courtship. Over the corpses and the bottles of formaldehyde and the tubes and pipes and the no-smell and the lowing of the dairy herd somewhere not so far away. And Evans loved the dead and he loved poor sad Muffled Myfanwy and he thought she might feel the same way, but it had not been so long since the hanging in the shed and the shuffle-board shooting in the back of the pub.

'And next we set the facial features. He does look like a grumpy bastard Myfanwy but we must think well of the Dead Dears. Now, we have closed the eyes; what a marvel that skin glue is and he was a stubborn one, Jones the Angry, so we used the flesh-colored eye caps, all oval, see? They sit on the eye and secure the eyelid in place and then a body can't argue with us. See how tidy that is? I closed his mouth and now *you* begin sewing his jaw shut. He'll be quieter, then. That's it. Come closer. Be firm with Jones. Take the suture string through the lower jaw below the gums, don't be timid as you go up and through the gums of the top front teeth. There you are Myfanwy, press hard with the needle; you can't hurt Jones now, although maybe some would say he deserved it, so poke it in hard and keep going. That's it. Lovely work. You learn so well, Myfanwy. A model student. Now there you are see, up into the right or left nostril and... no not down—*across*, like this.'

As Evans the Bodies took the needle to show her, they brushed arms and both felt a shiver and the warm smell of hope and happiness beyond the disinfectant, and then retreated. Myfanwy looked away. He passed the needle into her hand.

Rapture.

'That's it, across through the septum and into the other nostril and then back down into the mouth. Don't be shy. Push the needle like you mean it Myfanwy. There is such strength in your hands.'

Had he gone too far? He thought perhaps the compliment was too heavy for circumstance. Did the dead man mind? It was at this point that Evans the Bodies realised that he had, on this instance, failed to perform the death-checks. Jones seemed to have been stiff and then to have loosened up nicely at Myfanwy's loving touch, but maybe that was because he was stiff with hatred in life and was never touched so gently. No, he must be good. He'd submitted to the needle, so no need to palpate in the carotid artery. Evans knew that, in these modern times, people awakening on the preparation table was thought to be the province of the horror film, but he also knew that once Grim Peter from the old lighthouse had sat up to prevent his relieved relatives from celebrating that he was dead, how strong was his desire to catch them at it, hurl curses and deprive them of the fortune they knew he kept under the gargantuan pots of whitewash. There had barely been time for them to take the bunting down at the wake. But no, it was well. Present company didn't need to be palpated or double checked for cloudy corneas. And besides, Jones was always cloudy, always livid, barely alive in some ways. Evans looked at Myfanwy and considered her silent beauty.

'Then the two ends of suture string must be tied together. Do you have them there? Tie it neatly now and once you are sure you are secure with the jaw and he won't be dribbling, mould the mouth as you want it, now.'

Myfanwy nodded and tried to squeeze Jones's mouth into an enigmatic smile and Evans the Bodies shifted the giant silver tank for the embalming and began, visualising the draining arteries as he went, draining the blood from the body through the veins and replacing with his embalming solution via the arteries.

'That is a thing of strange beauty. Formaldehyde, glutaraldehyde, methanol, ethanol, phenol, and water, and I like it to contain a few dyes because we don't want our Dead Dears looking like alabaster. We want them to look like they've been on holiday, Myfanwy, even if I do sometimes have to pad them out a bit, like Dewi after he was hit with the spade that time or I'll later be showing you how to do with Mrs Morgan of the tractor accident.'

Myfanwy nodded. Drip, drip, drip, gurgle. Magenta, to clear and clean.

'Now begin your magic, Myfanwy.'

Myfanwy was now holding a bag in front of her. Now, she applied moisturising lotion to the face, lips, and hands, then powdered Jones on his face, neck, and hands in order to make him look less dead than dead and cover up his scorn-blown blemishes, discolorations and the seer marks of illness that he had hidden, even from himself. She gently applied powder to his body: 'For secreted oils, Myfanwy, but we won't go so far as to polish up his nails like we did for the Widow Williams, what with her liking the glitz and the men. And just brush his hair. Oh look Myfanwy. He makes a much better dead man than a live.'

Myfanwy gesticulated. What did she mean? Ah—he saw. Jones was wearing a toupée.

'Just stick it back on, my apprentice. I have some blu-tack for such events. There we are. Press it down on his head. And now, Myfanwy, is there is anything else of which we should take note, is it? Sometimes I don't know who is the student here and who is the apprentice. 'I mean to say'—again, had he gone too far?—'that you have a gift for the Dead Dears; it is lovely to see. But, as I was saying, has he come with a list? Does he want a cross or a special book? Is there any jewellery for the deceased?'

Again, Myfanwy gesticulated. A bag in the corner of the room, by the silver vats of blood and lymph and life force and the plastic containers of phenol and formaldehyde. 'Ah you thought of that, too. His belt with a tarnished silver buckle and the legend of his grandfather, Timothy the Nasty of Little Haven—oh the stories there are to tell—and photos of his cattle and his bird—she went to all the shows—and a picture of his chainsaws and a book. The Bible, of course? People like their Dead Dears to have The Bible even if they've been whores or accountants, Myfanwy.'

Evans the Bodies looked again.

'That I wasn't expecting: *THE COMPLEATE ANGLER* by Izaak Walton. It says 1653. How little we know. Did he want to be a gentleman fisherman? I didn't even know if he could read. Look you. *THE COMPLETE ANGLER OR, THE CONTEMPLATIVE MAN'S RECREATION.*'

Now, Evans the Bodies knew that the Dead Dears released surprises. In life, we could not always tell if a man read; if he recited poetry every night or chapters from *The Mabinogi* to his nasty cat. An examined, deep and cultured life was not always revealed to the outside world, perhaps if the owner of those things felt they were more brilliant kept separate and apart; or he was ashamed because his family laughed at literature and effete, delicate things—thought them unmanly or unworthy; something for a stumbling, decadent Englishman, when here, now, should only be the simple words of command and desire; of shopping and betting: of curse and television. But Evans had seen more: old texts about the Dead Dears' hobbies: once, from a budgie fancier and potboy, Jim the Fish, he found a burgundy leather copy of *THE NATURAL HISTORY OF CAGE BIRDS. THEIR MANAGEMENT, HABITS, FOODS, DISEASES, TREATMENT, BREEDING, AND THE METHODS OF*

CATCHING THEM by J.M. Bechstein, M.D. Of Walterhausen in Saxony. 1812 was given as the first printing and, below an exquisite plate of a golden oriole, he was lost in time as he learned about ornamental cages and diseases called The Pip, The Rheum, costiveness and The Bloody Flux; for the consumptive cage bird, the suggested remedy was the juice of a turnip. Evans had wanted to read to the end of the book and understand its beauty and barbarism, but the Dead Dears should not wait and no-one wanted to see Jim the Fish, because he had been bought from and dealt with—had the best crabs this side of the Neyland Bridge—but he had been unloved, so burial would not be halted and he would be laid to rest, this secret bird scholar, the intimacy of which was only known to Evans. And to me, of course, who saw everything and thought I might visit the man who wrote the book to see how he cradled the oriole before he wrest it from his world.

In time. Visit Jim the Fish as a young man; Jones the Angry. Give them kindness and see what that awakened.

Now, Evans the Bodies flicked gently through the new old book belonging to the dead man on the table—and he stopped, arrested at a single page containing a poem; he thought it must be a poem because it was smaller and narrower than the continuous writing. Things that were truncated were not description or stories, were they? He read the text aloud, stumbling, to Myfanwy, all the while held in time, like Jones on the slab under the turning pages, for reasons he did not yet comprehend:

But I will tell you some things of the monsters, or fish, call them what you will, that they breed and feed in them. Pliny the philosopher says, in the third chapter of his ninth book, that in the Indian Sea, the fish called Balaena or Whirlpool, is so long and broad, as to take up more in length and breadth than two acres of ground; and, of other fish, of two hundred cubits long; and that in the river Ganges, there be Eels of thirty feet long…

My God, Myfanwy, there is aqueous magic in this old book! Stories of Solan geese and laughing dolphins and massive, massive creatures. And look—I do love poetry, girl—he has here a poem from that splendid fellow George Herbert. Priest man he was, Montgomery on the Marches way he was born. Descended from the same stock as the Earls of Pembroke, so I like to think he's a Pembrokeshire lad. You know, when I am lonely, I do read from the poetry. Look, see. I didn't expect it here, but even in death there is song; there is lyric. Here, Mr. George Herbert his divine *Contemplation on God's Providence.*

Lord! who hath praise enough, nay, who hath any?
None can express thy works, but he that knows them;
And none can know thy works, they are so many,
And so complete, but only he that owes them.

'Oh Myfanwy, who would have thought it? Oh Myfanwy, what else is there to learn? Jones, nasty, cruel-tempered Jones. Angry as an artful angler with his old book, a secret gentleman and this poet.'

Evans's throat stop was loosed.

'And did he know the Lord—exact, transcendent and

divine? The discourse of rivers! How beautiful that is! And what is there to teach you. What book should I or could I write for you, Myfanwy. What of Jones's end, now in the coffin, the casket as some call it, which contains the body if it's going to be buried or entombed or as a means of burying cremated bits and it's a respectful and attractive way to transport the body before the burial or cremation but you know that, my beautiful silent woman, because you know everything! Do I tell you now that we learn how coffin materials are a matter of style for how can there be a material that can preserve a body forever and no material that will give you a better journey to the life hereafter? Oh Myfanwy, my love, coffins are also available in alternative materials, such as bamboo, willow, woven banana leaf, and pressed cardboard, among other materials and things they call alternative materials and green things. *Green*, my love, my only. But there is not much call for them in these parts. Oh but we can provide a half or full, which refers to whether the lid comes in two pieces or one piece and that in the case of a viewing, like with Jones, because his family want to know he's truly gone. So that they can drink and celebrate and go out on the boats and cheer, there will be a visitation and there must be full because all of him will be on display for his beloveds to gloat on the Dead Dear.'

Evans the Bodies and Muffled Myfanwy hefted Jones from the embalming table to the coffin, now waiting on the trolley next to it.

'Shift him with me, Myfanwy. I know you are strong. Do

not be shy that you have the strength of ten men and ten of your husband and son who left you so alone! And him in his shed like that, above all those fine garden tools. And him in the back room of the pub like this and being found by Llinois as he was and she only just a woman and what did she know of heartbreak or gunshot? I'm sorry Myfanwy'—she was crying now—'but I can keep it in no longer. I want to sing of what I feel and the Dead Dears I know. And I will teach you, like the only poem I know, about the pretty liners Myfanwy, the fabric lining the inside of the coffin which is all in my catalogue—look see; I have it here—which is sold to us puncture-resistant and leak-proof, and is made from satin, or velvet and oh—how I favour the very materials and start from the prick and static of the polyester and the electricity, Myfanwy, oh—electricity indeed.'

Evans the Bodies moved a step closer to Myfanwy.

'And there are commemorative panels, which are embroidered on the interiors of the coffin lid because some like it, and a special thing called internal lift hardware, which tilts the inside of the coffin up so that in a full or open, the body may be viewed at an angle. I am the only man in this part of Pembrokeshire to have such a thing. Myfanwy, oh Myfanwy, there is a thing in my catalogue called a memory tube, not because the dead remember, and not as if the atoms of the dirt and clay need to remember, but if we, silly living world, forget and if something should happen to the Dead Dears—should the coffin be dislodged from its space in a mausoleum or crypt, or unearthed from the ground, in apocalypse or great strife or a new housing development for people from away like that one on the Milford Road, then the identity of the Dead Dears can be easily known and we do not have to exhume them. Exhume. *Ex-hume. Ex-hale… Exquisite*—oh you smell of the sweetest summer meadow my beautiful Myfanwy! Oh God, my God, oh Jesu and the clifftop Virgin!'

And Evans the Bodies fell at her feet and worshipped at her knees and Jones lay silent and sewn up in his best suit. And then I, Almost, came forward from the twilight shadows at the edge of the room and I said, with a commanding voice that came up from the deep, a place I was only just beginning to understand, *Speak again, Myfanwy. Philip and Lewis the Younger Llewhellin want you to be free now. Speak Myfanwy! Cry and let go, for here is love in this strange barren place.*

And the greater stop was loosed from Myfanwy's throat and she said, 'Yes, Evans the Bodies and thank you and can you take me to chapel afterwards?' And she kissed him and was altered.

'Ynghanol ein bywyd, yr ydym yn angau,' she said, as she wept.

'Yes, Myfanwy: in the midst of life we are in death and here with the Dead Dears it is fair to say that we are in love.'

And there was another book that had only been seen by its owner, or nearly so.

Now.

Evans the Bodies wrote poems. Often for the Dead Dears who had no-one and whose lives must, he thought, be recorded for posterity. And there had been no-one there to toss his scribblings out, as Perfection or Miss Davies would have done for me, or for Seren. I was alive to all written down. So, in his book, the timid lady from the post office, who had customers and bread but no friends and a mother who would have tossed her out with the peelings for the pigs, became a cowslip in a warm meadow and drank deep of the sun and was happy; so a coarse and crooked man, who lived in the last house before St Brides Bay and whose children hated him but sang like larks for his money, was limned as a quiet man, skimming stones on the beach and smiling into the auroras of a coastal morning when no-one knew. But Evans the Bodies was a watcher for the sad and lonely. He was a dresser of bodies, to be sure, but he also had a talent for the sad soul and the lonely. And he had always loved Myfanwy; when she was someone else's, as she laboured for and lost her child, when both times he bought her milk-white lilies and she said, 'Evans, there's a soft man you are' and he cried with his back to her, as he did when she lost her husband. He put poems in the book for her, too. Imagined he was taking pictures of her, watching her written into the world all around and, as he watched the frosty lines on the windows in his cold parlour and saw the feathers and curlicues of winter, he scratched her monogram and, again, he cried, and imagined himself at a window as the beautiful ship Myfanwy his Love sailed away and thus he wrote *this*. I had seen it of course, but he did not know. I had learned it by heart and whispered it into the Pembrokeshire night, whose kind tendrils carried it to her and caressed her, then softly laid waste to her sadness and silence and made her think clearly about Evans the Bodies, who loved her and always had, just so. And he would not ever leave her, for when their very mass of atoms disassembled and went off to abide in rock pools and grains of sand, he was sure that theirs would still mingle, up there in the headland graves. So it went, for her…

Myfanwy , as you were: bay window, a side light and a black background.
Then as you were again: middle room—direct front light. I was specific.
Myfanwy—I was *precise; exacting* with the fall of dark and bright: I wrote it down.
Myfanwy, as I hoped you were. But you smiled and sailed away, sassy girl.

I sat for hours as the shadows fell, knowing what night must still portend: my craft.
drew a nail across a pane and scratched your name, invisible to others as
the evening settled in. I knew that morning brought a monogram in window frost
for you to see and I to know: I showed you how its feathered lines and confidence
spoke truth to us—that you could stay. The frost had crept along the span
to show you how this foolish clot had mouthed the most that could be said.

And then I spoke—and ruined all. A foolish joke: my love; my word—
Myfanwy, stay. Myfanwy, do not sail away.

I tried to draw another length to keep you here: pellucid worlds for us to share,
yet how I knew what I had done. You did not care for crystal casts,
the shapes recorded day by day. The metaphor for heavenly plan
was lost for you in my chapped hands—and so I scratched and tried to show
some better words to keep you here—to stall you with this simple moss-grown fool,
Why, no. Don't go, Myfanwy—stay. Myfanwy, do not sail away.

Myfanwy, yours, Evans, who loved you so since I first clapped eyes on you, girl, that cold night when they set off the fireworks from the castle for the Christmas lights. But I will wait a lifetime and set out fireworks when you are mine and then only.

And again, Myfanwy said, 'Yes Evans, bach, yes. And even in the midst of death we are in life and so we are in love.'

6

Perfection is besmirched

Ah life, death, buried, misplaced: all a jumble, to me. Some days, as a child, I went to the library in town, laughed at by the other boys after school, and I read and I read and I found old Welsh poems and there was this, marked Peredur Son of Efrawg—from The *Mabinogi*—and the lines went so:

...A tall tree on the river's bank, one half of it
burning from root to top, the other half in green leaf.

That is how it was and is with my heart; love and war; perfection and sin; sacrament and the kiss of a mermaid; death and life: love and death, as it was for Myfanwy and Evans the Bodies. Sudden; incongruous: deep sea and beaching. Love and death; life and death. All and one. I am telling you more than one story. But as I was saying, beside the green-leaved, burning tree in scant picnics at Capel Dewi, up at Walton

West, I felt alone and sad: but the happiness would come. I thought this. If you're dragged up Welsh, or perhaps even half so, I do believe that your thought's often in poetry. You can't help it. So,

In this drear place, I see my family loved
in celandines and mugwort garlands drawn;
I do not know what tears or mossy lies
they fought so hard to keep from being said.
Llewhellins, thick and fast and tired and gone, their stories drawn in stone or footstep sand.

I never heard more of the ragged man and on I worked with Evans the Bodies, getting older both; breathing all the more sensual and deep, I. Longing for the beautiful, terrible kiss of my mermaid girls. Thinking of Seren, my star. Back at our home, Charity House, Perfection brutally attacked the furniture, as my mother had taught her to do. There were hard, mean ways you could scrub and polish and also ways that you could cook to punish. But here, beside Nabob and the spiteful cooking and cleaning, was love. If my mother had given me a name to aspire down to, then what of hers? She was a dumpy woman; squat legs and thick waist and no discernible shape to her lower face. Her eyes were sort of high tide colour, her skin the colours on a razor clam and her nose was formless. Her red hair had its beauty and yet her features, taken individually, if not lovely, were at least interesting. She had an anagram of a good face, which I think, like 'No Man is an Island', came from *The Mabinogi*.

But love is not linear, circular or logical. And so when someone came for her, and took her from me, I needed to find out who it was and propel them into the past because I loved her and I loved her.

Perfection was praying to Mary, or at least our version of her, with the pipe and the rolled up sleeves and the harassed look from being the Mother of Jesus and the Holy Queen and from doing all that when she wasn't technically omniscient and omnipresent and oh—the intercessions were exhausting and back and back and back to her came all the pain in the world.

'Holy Mary, Speak to the Lord Jesus for me!'

Was Mary saying, 'Yes, now, in a minute. I am doing something!'

And Perfection was praying to her.

'Mary, Mother of God, I am not a religious woman, but help me as you spoke to my grandmother Bronwen and my great grandmother, Eleri and you helped them and stopped them murdering their husbands and let their cakes win in the show and didn't let on, through your Holy Grace, Mary Mother of Jesus, Blessed Virgin, that they powdered the onions in talcum and dipped the eggs in tea for the same and you helped Eleri cover up all her indiscretions with the men at the pub and all.'

Silence.

'Mary, Blessed Virgin, are you very busy right now? Are you talking to the Llewhellin men about the hangings and shootings and to dead Mrs Morgan about all the illegitimate children she had with the men down the Milford tankers, especially Ted from Panama?'

Silence.

'Mary, speak to the Lord Jesus for me? I am sad. I am married to a man who does not desire me and the people in the village do not like me and I take no pleasure in beating my brother and in Nabob, but I feel compelled. And I think I have turned into Mammy, all the beatings with a hairbrush, but I'm not beautiful like her. And the sea taunts me and the kelp threatens to drown me and I look at the deep pools on the beach and I think about drowning myself in them, which is a sin. There is so much hanging and shooting and misplacing. I don't want to be a Llewhellin like them.'

Silence.

'Oh, Perfection Llewhellin!'

'She speaks to me!' Yet the tone was sneering and didn't sound like Our Lady.

But now came, with the sneer, a laugh, biting and black, like, and the virgin was silent and up the Acheronian path came the dark form, taunting. It cursed Perfection, my sister, and beat her and she was silent in the gloaming and could pray to Our Lady no more. In the darkness the sordid eyes gleamed. I was out on the beach and I heard her cry and saw their gleam and felt the profanity of them and was sick. These were eyes that loathed the world. I ran to her. She had tried to beat him off with Nabob; she had hit out with the poker and the loaf of bread and the knife and the board and all that she could reach. She tried to speak, but could not and when she looked at me, her eyes looked not at this present plane but at something in the future where she could be safe. Be happy. I wanted to take her there, just as I would propel the keeper of those eyes into the sea-past and coffin him there.

From that day, she was muffled and could never speak or tell us what she had seen. She rocked shut against the sea and us and the world. From the corner of the room I thought I heard Mammy curse her from the life beyond for not being stronger and able to beat him off—I say *him*; I felt—I knew—it was a him. I hated Mammy for not nurturing her girl and coming to her when she was bleeding and a weakling. She hadn't come in life; she didn't come in near-death and she should have done for how did the difference matter? I tried to think that my mother was, for her own reasons, too scared while I sat with Perfection and stared into her life-dead eyes and tried to kindle a spark there, as we waited for Dr Morgan the Pints. Oh, why would someone hurt her? She was spiteful and hateful and cursed and had no friends for her temper, but everyone knew that: she had got it all from her mother. There was nothing, I thought then, of value in our house and had there been, why not come when Perfection was out as the back door was always laid open through poor housekeeping or a window generously ajar? What reason could there be to hurt her so?

Up the path lurched Dr Morgan the Pints, fresh from The Sloop. Around here, where things could be up in the air and backwards forwards, we turned a blind eye. Morgan was kind and careful as he prescribed, in his cups.

'Beaten is it? Terrible. The second time tonight, this.'

'The second time?'

'Yes. Owen on the harbour, going for a night dive. Someone came from behind him. They found him knocked and bleeding on the rocks. We have sent him to Carmarthen. Terrible, terrible things. Hold her hand now, boy.'

I did. Her hand, in mine, clutched dearly, although her eyes were glassy and elsewhere, like the Dead Dears in Evans's parlour.

'Now Perfection. I will ring for an ambulance and you must come with us. Don't cry boy. You are nearly a man now and your sister may not be the same as before and will need you. She may turn out simple now.'

Dr Morgan the Pints was kind, but it was fair to say that he treated the ill and injured as if they were dead and blind and not able to hear his pronouncements of radically reduced expectations. Evans the Bodies was more tactful with the Dead Dears.

We sat, as the sea moaned. It was the end of Christmas; the last day of the tree and the twinkling lights on the headland. Perfection was taken away by the ambulance and the house went quiet and I thought hard. I put her things in order; placed her comb and mirror and her little dictionary on the windowsill and, on top of them, I placed Nabob. She would be my sister, simple or not. And I wanted the things there to remind me of the blood revenge which I must take; I was the only one who could, though Perfection and Morgan the Pints could hardly know it. And when Rhys came in, with news of Owen on the Rocks (as his name rapidly became), to our new life here, I saw him weep, then straighten. And we followed Perfection to Carmarthen where she was looked at and prodded and talked to with no result; and where her eyes stayed glassed over and the doctor told us her head would not be the same and that sometimes the shocked and hurt were shocked and hurt beyond words and it could be her poor brain or it could be a mutism rocking shut against the world, or perhaps selective so she might speak to us.

I said, and I should not have, 'But when she speaks it is mainly to curse.' And the doctor shot me a disgusted look and wrote something in the notes, but Rhys smiled because he knew the curses yet, as I said, love is not linear, circular or logical.

We left her there for the swelling had to come down and she was fitting then, and it was not a pretty sight.

But one day she came home and sat, from then on, at the window, looking out across the sea like Muffled Myfanwy had done. Say what you like about Perfection, she was mostly an inept worker, but she had been a hard one. And our household needed her. So, into the house, in time, came Gwyneth to help us. To wash and clean and help Rhys with the shop and its goods and accounts and make sure I did my homework. Evans the Bodies gave me written assignments because it was a proper apprenticeship, like, with the Dead Dears, and I doing my embalming training. When Evans set his assignments, the assessor in Haverfordwest often reworded them because Evans wrote as he spoke. 'Care and

Management of the Body' was fine; 'Mortuary Fashion', 'Trends for the Dead Dears' and 'How to Embalm, is it' were not.

But as I was saying, sometimes I was lazy and distracted and, truly, elsewhere too, and Gwyneth retrieved me and made sure I did my work. She had delicate hands, a lightness of tread that, after Perfection's heavy feet, made her seem almost invisible. She was pretty surrounded by the motes of dust and she was the only person we ever saw Perfection smile at. It was true: we saw our sister and wife smile with her eyes at Gwyneth, which was a blessing we had never seen before. Her mouth smile had been broken by our mother's sour tongue, nasty brass on the palate, and her train of thought ruptured by her attack that night. But with Gwyneth her eyes lit up, losing their sad glassy quality: a special smile; a gentle touch of the hand. But Perfection never spoke, though Gwyneth understood her.

But it was wrong. I would find the attacker. I, Almost, would track him down. And, if I could, the man who left old Llewhellin in the mound of violets, or the man on the rocks. I sensed the same hand. Then I would propel this person into a past that he could not understand and in which he would be slowly destroyed as an anomaly, an unwanted true anachronism. I would do that with a story, once I found him. You see, oh my fine tender friend, I was starting to understand what I was capable of.

7

Far stranger than Wales

Do you know girl, that there are those who do not understand how the landscape speaks to us? How, when we know it and allow it to know us, that natural world—a twilight sea world, the damp sea cave or the crawling salt-mud of the estuary—instructs us how to prevail. Here are some lines, committed to memory of course, that I made when I needed protection. And maybe even the angry dead come for one of their own, in a better place now they are. So I compressed this thought of mine into another poem.

Today we will go inland dear, to see the rhododendron bloom,
Away from sea scent, sunset shell; away from me, away from you.
We travelled for hours on little tracks, their way being marked with showy prime,

It was, at first, of some delight, but then my love spoke of his crime:
So stay here, love, forever held, unless you scent the estuary,
And I fly high, to England bold, away from you, away from me.
Oh bach, you underestimate my knowledge of this mazèd land,
You did not hear the laughing breeze, dead Mammy's come and with her hand
She'll pen you up, beside the Rhos, and I will run forever free,
I'll not stay here, forever held, not stay with you but live for me—
An orient boat will rescue me, blown on dead Nanny's pretty curse
And rhododendron casket blooms will strip your life and end my verse.

I see I may have startled you. Perhaps I will continue to do so.

More work of the dead.

More words on the Dead Dears.

Magic: *Celtic magic.*

Matthew Arnold wrote about it, you know, in Victorian times, when he wasn't being disinterested, like; it's that precarious, strong, dissolving, holding mood of two things at the same time: of love and hate; fight and the gentlest caress; a beautiful, *beautiful* linking of things we suppose to be incongruous. But we are wrong. From the headland and the brine, we are metaphysicals. Think on this, girl: '…a tall tree by the side of the river, one half of which was in flames from the root to to the tip, the other half was green and in full leaf' from *The Mabinogi.* How can that be, you might say? This is how life and death are. That is how we laugh when *you* might not; why we might love in a strange, barren place, like Evans the Bodies and his hitherto silent witness.

In the midst of life we are in death: *ynghanol ein bywyd, yr ydym yn angau.*

So, I continued my apprenticeship with Evans the Bodies. I learned to sew and suture and use the eye caps and I learned, also, the two sorts of embalming. Evans said it was in case I could go international with it, like; Bristol way. I told you about the arterial embalming, but there is another kind, called cavity embalming and for that, Evans gave me a special silver tool called a trocar and he had had my name engraved on it. I learned, like a surgeon, to make a small incision near the belly button and then I would put the trocar in the cavity. I always winced at that word—the cavity—but then, we are all vessels, filled only with soul and that soul animates us and gives us so much more power than you could ever have guessed at. I would remember this as I used my trocar, on the organs in the chest cavity and abdomen while I punctured them and drained each of gas and fluid contents—the Dead Dears would sigh and bubble sometimes and I would soothe them and talk to them, as I had watched Evans doing, and Myfanwy, too, when I had given her back her voice and she had spoken words of love.

'Mrs Roberts, do not be sad. Now you are with Evans and

Myfanwy and Almost and we will take care of you. And your soul is in the life hereafter and you can see Mr Roberts and Gelert the dog and your mother on the side. Just try not to sigh too much as we puncture,' said Evans the Bodies, '—and also I have a feeling that Mr Roberts's mistress is not where *you* are going but in The Other Place; down The Primrose Way, as they say.'

And when I had carved and punctured, the organs would be replete with the fluids from Evans's vats of formaldehyde-based chemical mixtures. And I learned to sew with the catgut: I closed the incision and I said a silent prayer for the Dead Dears and hoped they would forgive me for the sharpness of what I had done and, in a way, thanked my sister Perfection for all the evenings she spent thrashing me with Nabob until my darning and sewing were good enough to make me a proper man and stop the Dead Dears from mewling and dribbling.

At home, Perfection sat by the window, mostly, and did not speak and Gwyneth kept a tidy home. When she was needed in the shop, she would wheel my sister down talking to her all the while. Perfection looked not at Rhys, who had never desired her, but at Gwyneth, who cared for her with delicacy. And always she told Perfection of her times outside their home and of its wildlife, moods and seasons.

'The puffins will be in their burrows on Skomer. Oh—that is a beautiful sight, all those cheeky little birds. Yesterday, I walked on the beach and I thought I saw a thousand crab shells and three hundred jellyfish all washed up, poor things.

And the boys were flying kites, but I walked until I was alone and I found you the most perfect pebble on the beach, Look, see.'

A perfect white oval pebble, for Perfection, who cradled it in her hand, and smoothed it gently, like the face of the alabaster beauty of a baby she would never have. And a tear rolled down her cheek.

'Oh I have upset you. Let's get to the shop. We'll have tea there and Rhys will be so pleased to see you, yes?'

It wasn't Perfection Rhys most loved to see now, but her carer, who would paint with him in his pastels, after hours, when the beauty of the colours would spread up their arms and into their hearts.

But my life here would come, for a while, to an end. Evans the Bodies had taught me well and after four years in his tutelage, a dark man, called Mr Williams, who, it was said, inhabited a strange mansion off a motorway near London, sent word that I should come to see him. And I did. I went to his polished, sterile world, more dead than the Dead Dears and I saw, chairs never brushed with fingertips and an immaculate fridge and coffee table. I saw posed cardboard people in pictures on the wall and big extravagant boxes of accounts and I was out of sorts there.

'I am a lawyer,' said Williams, 'and I sent word to your Godforsaken part of the country that you are to be rich and have inherited a fortune.'

Williams's voice was ecstatic at the very mention of money. Its two syllables dripped with filthy sexual things:

not pure and pretty sexual things, like the breasts of my mermaids, but consumptive, conspicuous imbibing and eating of the heart and cruel expectation and want and heat. He was posh; but he was a sewer rat. He was not glad for me; he was aroused by rolling the oily words—rich; money; fortune—around his mouth. I did scent a Welsh burr in that voice; intriguing, but loathsome in his jaws, if so. He'd gone English, for shame.

'The benefactor is, at least to you, anonymous but the enormous amount of money you are to inherit will mean that you can be elevated from caressing dead people in your Godforsaken milking parlour to the Temple and I shall be your mentor.'

'But who *is* the benefactor?'

'That, boy, I am not permitted to share with you.'

I knew it was Miss Davies and that maybe the gentle whispers of my mermaids had made her put aside some considerable wealth for me so that I could travel and do all sorts. I was sure of it.

'Are you some sort of priest—at the Temple?'

'Feeble boy. I can tell you're not without sense or ability. And you have providence and wealth on your side, so you are elevated from a cipher in my eyes; you are standing in rich place! That is Shakespeare, although you would not know!' (*Ah, but I did.*) 'But the things you people do not know! The Temple. It is hallowed ground, alright. It is where you practise law, you little fool.'

I was still confused. But I didn't want to be with this sewer rat, however much he promised of expectations for me. I wanted to travel and to be with the Dead Dears. Maybe the English ones. Or to have my own place. Almost the Bodies. That was it.

'I do not want to practise law, Sir, I want to look after the Dead Dears.'

'The Dead Dears? Good God! But then, not Good God for as you must surely know, God does not exist! Death is death and why should you care as you shuffle them off and burn them?'

I felt this was just about the most horrible thing I had heard a man say. I was going to be sick, or faint like a silly girl at heartbreak. But instead I composed myself, as Evans the Bodies had taught me to do, especially to do in the saddest cases and I said, 'Sir, they are going to The Life Hereafter and I have learned how to care for them. It's my craft. It's my art. I learned it well. I know its moral codes and all its ways.'

'Moral codes? The law *is* morality you fool and it has nothing to do with God. The universe is an accident but everything on that accident is man-made and all you can be sure of is a book or rules and the money you make.'

'Sir, that is not a life for me.'

Williams looked at me in utter derision, then he laughed. 'Let me read this to you, boy. Let me tell you the pleasure of wealth.' Williams coughed and picked up his collection of Ben Jonson's plays, 'Attend!'

A ROOM IN VOLPONE'S HOUSE. ENTER VOLPONE AND MOSCA.

VOLP: Good morning to the day; and next, my gold: Open the shrine, that I may see my Saint.
Quite! Look at this sensible, happy man.
Hail the world's soul, and mine! more glad than is
The teeming earth to see the long'd-for sun
Peep through the horns of the celestial Ram
Am I, to view thy splendour darkening his;
That lying here, amongst my other hoards,
Shew'st like a flame by night…

'Do you attend, boy? I admire Volpone's cunning purchase of his wealth; that all his gain is not by common way! You people out West. Simpletons. Do you never yearn for cleverness and guile? The world is not kind and it will defeat a simpleton. So glorious, boy! The skill of this fox and his friend!'

…But, you see, I was a reader and knew that the fox and the the fly—the cunning little parasite—were eventually consigned to prison and slave galley. And I thought, though he saw me as rough and uneducated, that he was a man of mean culture who never read to the ends of books, but lifted and deployed quotations that summed up his life and wants; he took the words and exploited them greedily, as he saw fit. He would have been an excellent candidate for Jonson's fun. Not so much a*vocato* or *avocatore*, but *sanguisuga*; the leech;

bloodsucker. This characterisation I kept to myself. Bastardy. *Parasit.*

'I think, Sir, that I want to be like Evans the Bodies, instead.'

The man showed me the door. 'Do as you will. This world has little meaning and no-one cares for you or for the dead. It's your gold and cunning that make sense. But you still have you benefactor and I will still administer your accounts while you squander your fortune with your ugly corpses.'

I said (he didn't understand): 'I am more John Donne than Jonson in impulse sir. Out of the headland you would despise, we are metaphysicals.'

'Fool,' he said.

But what did he know? I, bookworm. Traveller. *Boyo.*

I left London, changed at Temple Meads and set out for Clandestine House. I felt sullied by Williams and his concupiscent dripping and, for a while, less full of hot blood than I should be from my encounter. I dreaded that I must see the man again. But beyond Kidwelly, a fair breeze drew through the windows and the tang of salt cleaned my skin and made me hopeful of something fresh and unclouded and where a sanguisuga would fall from the skin like sadness from a loved child, breaking into his run on a summer beach under the Perseid meteor showers.

And where a good man called Rhys would find a love that filled the world all around and reached back into the past and healed that too. It's possible, don't you know?

How, Almost? That's what you want to know, isn't it?

Well, now, *te*: I was coming to that.

8

The House

Clandestine House was silent, but up the mossed path I went. I whistled and my girls came to me, Dilys and Nerys.

'Almost? How troubled you look!'

And before I could gain the front door, my girls took me to the ebb and flow of the water and I was washed by the waves and their mouths kissed me better and I felt their rapture and their heartbeats in my limbs and loins and, for a while, I was whole.

'That is our boy and this is our world. Kiss us again, Almost.'

And I did and I did, for the kiss of the mermaid is pure and it is not for sex, but is clean and delicate and its heat is sacred. And when they washed me up on the pebbles as the Cleddau roused itself to turn back through the woods and was happy, I asked them to go with me, in their other forms, to the house. To see Miss Davies and understand the money and the future she hoped for me; to see Seren and feel her scorn when I loved her and I loved her and I always had and always would.

I expect you are wondering this: *but Almost, what of the incident just now with the mermaids if you felt yourself so devoted to Seren?*

To this, I would say that you misunderstand the nature of this world, its lusts and fevers and you don't know yet about those of the world you cannot see—the *worlds* you cannot see. But suspend your disbelief. And also, I hope you feel the confidence in my voice and that my stern eye has made you see that you should trust to do me this. Suspend it, then, your disbelief, realising that hours have gone and that you are suspended, also, in time. And thus is my power now. But I must continue your story!

So Dilys took the form of the harvest mouse and scuttled behind me, eyes bright, and Nerys was a sleek otter, venturing from the water further than the natural and we were together and cooler now once we stepped out of the bath of heat. And oh, we were friends.

It was a bright day, but the house, as ever, basked in the sepulchral and I walked down its path, it felt like the keenest brightness came from the eyes of my friends. But they scuttled to the side of the house to watch and I rang the bell. Seren answered. She glowered at me, but she was so very beautiful.

'Been away, is it?'

'Yes, I have been hearing of news from Miss Davies but I need to hear it from her.'

'I don't know what you are talking about, but then nothing in the world makes sense to me, Almost.'

Did she smile at me, almost?

Miss Davies was enthroned in the gloaming and I could see that, yet again, the furniture had been rearranged and that the pictures were different. Different cardboard-posed people; I may even have recognised some of them from other people's families and lives. Never did they really have anything to do with Miss Davies, but as my girls had explained to me, she created her reality new each time. It came to me—and I don't know why it had not before—that she did this because her true life and the things that might have happened to her (some of which I knew and of which I already told you) might have so painful that it was not possible for her to feel them, so to construct, in her near darkness, an alternative narrative was the only palatable thing. To see herself as an invalid who would crack like old parchment in bright sunlight meant that she would not venture out; perhaps the physical pain she ascribed to herself was not so real as the torment in her mind: she had decided to replace one with another. For the first time, I wondered whether the clawed hand of Miss Davies, raking my back as it always did, could straighten and flex with daylight and with joy. Could I heal her with a story?

'Almost, come here.'

'So I met Williams.'

'Who?'

Did she wink? Did her sad eyes acknowledge the name? She croaked, 'I do not *quite* know who you mean, Almost.'

Quite.

'Miss Davies, I know that you do.'

'I know that I do not.'

'But I know that you do!'

'An otter—at the window!' This was Seren, eyes shining, like the creature, seeing clams and sea urchins, its favourites.

'A harvest mouse—on the sill!' This was Miss Davies.

In her eyes I saw no knowledge and I did not think she could pretend because all the strength of her pretence was taken up with the management of her own carefully constructed vision of home, past and present. It was not her and if not her, then whom? Who cared for me so? And who needed to keep it secret and employ a leech to deliver news of it?

The otter and the harvest mouse looked at me, ill-concealed this time, then ran for the quay, watched by the two women. Then they were gone, my girls, out to the green, tails flashing

Seren showed me to the door. Star. Fixed luminous point. Remote incandescence. Auger, but of what? Perfection's auger shell. I began to feel a pattern brimming behind my eyes. The house on the quay breathed and the moss outside the front door crept over my toes, and the rocks of the sea bed, my girls told me, respired and wept. It was all alive, but it was my mission to live for the Dead and, whoever had funded my living, be blessed and cursed for their secrecy. And this landscape be blasted for not giving up the secrets of its sadness. Or that is, not yet, girl.

9

The English

I saw some very personal writing once, in public and when I was very much younger. A slip of paper by the door of the harbour shop at Little Haven on St Brides Bay. At first I thought it was romantic; like you would. But then, melancholy boy, I thought it would have another narrative sewn onto it. And I was right. A girl walked into the sea, came up on the tide where the sea cave of Little Haven calls to its cliff cousins at Broad Haven. Her. Never wait for happiness. Claw it; catch it; don't leave it a note for later, however pretty it is trimmed up. Of course, I made it pop in a poem. Committed to memory, not scraps.

In the old shop on the harbour walk I saw a note: Be Mine:
were you that girl I saw on the sand, turning to face me
against the gale? I think you saw me and I want to know.
It was there for weeks, that note, rusting in the sun,

and brushed by arms of the boys running from the beach
for ice cream and the papers for bored parents.
And weeks more it hung, unnoticed, torn;
down in shreds it was, a girl could never see;
But a girl *had nothing seen*. She'd been looking instead
over the shoulder of the keen bright boy
to the brave tarred man who broke her heart: a challenge—
Find me, save me. Do not let me now walk out
into the sea. But in the keening of the wind
and the straining of the gale, all turned away
and she was gone and the slips of note removed,
for something clean and tidy and not sad.

And *I* had to be gone, too. Had to see elsewhere. Felt compelled. So now I had the money, I needed to run my own show, as they say. And I did not know where to go. I did not want to be in competition with Evans and I did not want to be in London or have anything to do with the world of the big motorway or the precious gated community world where Williams lived. I did not want his law or his kind of temple. So where, is it? Could I bear to be away from the sea and from the estuary? From Seren, from the clawed hand raking my back? Could I bear to be away from Nerys and Dilys, my girls of the Cleddau and the bright dark world beyond, and the moss that crept and the stones that respired? I was not confident that this happened in other places and, you know, over the border. But I had a friend. He had done it; he was a boy who sometimes gave me the eye in school, oh yes, the eye. Just as I am now fluid in time, why should I not be so in other ways? Binary is not gorgeous. Great God, no.

Ned Owens was in Somerset, doing a business of sorts, and we spoke and he said there were possibilities for work here and that, although he did not know so many dead people and felt they were so much more active in our corner of Wales, still there was the possibility of business because always there were Dead Dears.

Oh I mourned when I left Perfection and Rhys; and I mewled into the brine when I was with my girls and they pulled me under the waves and bathed me in their heat and I remember the beads of it on their breasts, in the lavender kelp, and that the sea boiled around us and we gasped into each others' mouths and rose up upon the crests of waves and we were sorrowful and jubilant. But mermaids do not age like us; they are not immortal exactly, but their shine does not wear off and they are rosy cheeked perpetual and they carry their essential energy through centuries until their hearts are stilled and passed into their mermaid children and the water creatures that are their friends and harbingers to the unknowing and to those with whom they choose to make friends and who become their lovers. I see I have shocked you with my talk of all this, but as I said, their sex is like a chaste heat. There is nothing in it of want and concupiscence and grasping. It is pure. My girls said they would find a way to get to me as the oceans are unconfined. But I feared for them: the mud of the Bristol Channel is thick and deep. I worried they would stick and suffocate.

So I went. It was a place called Bath. I was told it was full of round streets and golden stone. A place of a thousand herring gulls with dry feet. The up and down road runs from St David's in a very straight line. In Haverfordwest, there are many roundabouts and a myriad cars and a stone circle almost absorbed into a supermarket car park, then, as you go further, Narberth and Llanddewi Velfri, where ancient uncles of mine, as Mammy used to say, kept their women, and a strange blind aunt fixed you with her cruel eye and you could not move from the spot as she rooted you like she had the power of a Preseli gorgon and underneath her cap were snakes; then you see that part of the Pembrokeshire National Park which they sold off, though they said they never would, to make a posh holiday resort mostly for the people from away and on this place, covered with little villas and facilities, stands the old Newton farm where my grandmother, Bronwen, was born. I expect she haunts them now, all the shrieking swimmers, piercing their feet like a weever fish as they swirl unselfconsciously through the unreal water. And Catherine, you see the purple mountains and out there near Nevern is Pentre Ifan, the dolmen where my father used to go and think, it was said, before he was misplaced, and then you are in Carmarthen, all stripped out at its heart by the new developments where my family used to bet and smoke pipes and walk down to the cattle market and my long-gone and whiskered matriarchs out-bid any men with both money and spirit. These places are made new, but they are all haunted. In the new builds at night, ancient dead people spit and stir and their very atoms unsettle the casual drinker in the pub or walker to the fancy hotels and tea rooms and places that do up old crafts and sell them as vintage. And you drive on and reach the big road and you glimpse Cardiff Bay and then I hoped my girls were bobbing out there beyond Steep Holm and Flat Holm islands and laughing. So on towards the sweeps of the Severn, the land of the 1605 tidal wave (oh, I went back to see that later) and the mud and the ammonites in its cliffs at Aust and their dangerous, terrible tides and oh, the bridge is like a soft green galleon, with its curves and sweeps of railing and wires like sails and it turns sensuously and then you land and it says *Croeso i Loegr* and your heart goes thump into your shoes and it is over and you're sad and you fancy yourself back just across the sweep of the river and then you are at home.

I am not a content traveller, but I tell my stories of people who travelled this way. And of Welsh feet and the old, vitriolic women of my family compelled to visit relatives in London. Bronwen knew Eltham and Plumstead and Greenwich with the big ship and then Lewisham, which they called Blackheath to be posh, and then the move out towards the suburbs and places I could not construe and where I never saw people in the streets and where my relatives had had no-one to talk to that was from Pembrokeshire. So you sweep up a valley, past the line of tall trees you can see from anywhere, and down another valley, through a place called Pennsylvania although I saw no woods there, just an angry narrow road bisecting a once-village, and away to your side sweeps the city in the bowl and it is fine, alright, but it is too alive and not haunted enough and I feared it would be as Ned Owens had said. It is old, but it is not properly so and it has been varnished and sanded. But oh! I had to try.

Croeso i Loegr.

I went to set up house in Bath, but I was nervous of the sweeps of yellow stone, to begin with. I had this money, so, at first, we went posh and found a place in The Circle. But there was something about its shape which unsettled me ever; and I needed a place with lower ceilings and tighter walls and the sense that people were not looking up at my lovely place, so I shifted from the city and Ned came with me. Seven miles away in Wiltshire was a place called Bradford on Avon; a congested town, to be sure, but we found an old house that used to be a pub and I could feel that it was steeped in old time proper, oily flagstones; in high fireplaces and conversation and bodies in the cellar and coffins through a hatch. It was a perfect, imperfect house and I had the notion, all Hobbit-like, that I could cosy up and make my way with the dead in this old house; and that all could come to an old pub—we were told it used to be The White Lion—and drink and be not sad. In my head it was as Bilbo, in my bed book, described Rivendell: *...a perfect house, whether you like food or sleep or story-telling or singing, or just sitting and thinking best, or a pleasant mixture of them all. Merely to be there was a cure for weariness, fear, and sadness.* When I closed my eyes, I made it thus: Imladris, house in an Elven town and the dwelling of Elrond, in Middle Earth—the 'last Homely House East of the

Sea'. At least that was my dream-hope and my day waking. It still is. I want your home to be like that; for you, my sad friend. It is simply a matter of tea and table and spirit, not of the belonging or emolument. But it is better in Wales, if you can now, girl. But you live now in the house which I describe and I am happy for that.

As I was saying, though, I had to make my way. Ned with me, setting up together. He'd had his boats on the canal and his nature walks and a little bit of teaching here and there because he was a bright one, Ned. No-one wanted to learn Welsh (a disappointment) and really he found the walks not so rugged as he would like and when he set up the coracles, like his great grandfather and his uncle in Llandysul, there were no takers apart from a lady who near drowned and so he took up with me and with the Dead Dears of Here.

'Ned, why now not be with the Dead if the quick don't like you so much?'

'You, lad, are a strange one, but I'll give it a go.'

Ned had a girl, too; Anna-Katrina and I will tell you more of her when I tell you more of Seren; in my heart, that sour beauty's spirit crossed the border with me, and I bet she knew it, damn her.

So the parlour. We couldn't operate what we must from the front room, now could we? But we had some money, now. Ned had been careful but, most of all, I had the money from whoever had gifted it to me. Still I sometimes thought it could be Miss Davies, though the clawed hand denied it. Now, I had my diploma just come through from

Pembrokeshire College and Evans the Bodies, so I could take on Ned as my apprentice and teach him to sew up nicely. There is much to think about, I discovered, when starting out in business. I got advice from Evans and oh how I missed him. He said to think of this, now: oh God I yearned, oh *hiraeth*, to hear his voice rattle and boom down the line, like the choir in church ringing on the very earth under the flagstones.

'Boy, you have to think of the location of a funeral home because it needs to be well for those who want to see the Dead Dears. First, you will need enough space for visitations and you have to have office space because, remember now Almost, the records are all important, is it. I've made some dreadful mistakes in my time. Jenkins of Nevern has for years been visiting his wife in the wrong place, but you won't tell I am sure. Now, boy: you will also need an area separate from the main showing area for embalming and cremation props and trinkets. Like our tables for Myfanwy and me, see? You can't be draining near the showing and we can't have trimming up and puffing round or buckets and tubes near the visited departments, although I've had a few spiteful relatives ask in my time. Remember me telling you about Timothy the Nasty of Little Haven? Asked to see his wife while we were preparing to check that she was really gone: "Timothy," I said, "I know you are grieving, but that is not a thing you you should do. It is not respectful."

"She was a thing of darkness," said he, "And I need to tell *Her* at The Sloop while the bed is unmade."

That was his mistress, of course, and now I say that to you again, I do see that circumstances and speech were a little suspicious—but we move on, boy, we move on. And as I was saying, finally, you two boys will need an area where coffins and clothes and the other bits and pieces involved in planning and decorating the funeral can be set up for display, see. Now that is something I always wanted at my place. Myfanwy (once my love could speak) told me quite firmly that we didn't need it, but I had always wanted a sort of gallery, or a shop; lovely things for sad times where you could choose your shade of crêpe, but Myfanwy, she said, "No that is morbid and a shade too far, Evans the Bodies," although she does let me have my velvet corner where I keep the Dead Dears' possessions: all the surprising books of beauty from the folk we think, in life, do not read. But we are wrong, Almost, wrong. We do not see inside their souls and you do not know the intellect of another if he will not speak. Now, finally pay attention to parking space but I am bound to say that you should not charge for parking. You remember the protests over that in Pembroke? And then you need think of how you will be moving the Dead Dears from your premises to the street for funeral processions.'

'So much, then, to think about!'

'Well I have more to say!' Evans the Bodies was declaiming again in his catalogue voice; that which had won Myfanwy, with my help, of course:

'Now the equipment you will need to run a proper job with the Dead Dears is going to cost thousands, Almost.

You remember me talking to you about this all? Keep a Ledger of Death, both. Now when I bought my embalming kit it came from that sour fellow in Carmarthen and it cost three thousand pounds. Do not go cheap, though. A good finish and a proper craftsmen's make are a proper send off, however bitten the corpse. Then, you'll be needing your embalming table and you mustn't skimp on build quality. That I learned to very poor disadvantage because when I was doing up Timothy the Nasty's wife, there was a merry tumble as he came in to gloat, see? So build quality is all, boy. You will need your refrigerated storage and really I should say hydraulic lifts, but then I finds Myfanwy and I can do most of that. I am a strong man for hefting and cradling my Dead Dears.

Have you thought out the rest? Are you thinking of offering cremation services, for then you'll need a cremation system as well, but we will talk more about this because it isn't my favoured way to go and, round here, we have plenty of turf, see? Places from away? Well, I expect that they are *that* crowded, so look into it all? Or go unofficial and see if they can quietly push them up a bit for room, like, in the burial ground. You could consider the memory tubes I used to talk about. They will be in the catalogues. Best to make sure who's who. Now your products: you should know all this, but caskets, clothing embalming fluid, hairdressing and make-up and urns if you are providing cremation services. Oh there are beauties in my catalogues, as I have told, and don't forget the full or the partial: is the Dead Dear to be seen or obscured? With the memory tubes and all, little pieces of delicacy, boy. Now, the cost of these items can vary and you must be calm but hard headed: you must negotiate the best price possible and that isn't wrong through you're not on the market bargaining for fish. And you have to think of your furnishing: I am told there is a thing called shabby chic, but that is not it at all for your proper work. You want plain, tidy chairs to keep grieving loved ones comfortable and content those who are pretending to grieve or even slightly pleased. A small table is good in case tea is required but I should add that, in our business, it is vital, Almost, *vital*, to keeps urns and receptacles separate and apart or all Hell will break loose if you make tea with the wrong thing. If you are having hot drinks, then in my view coasters are also important because mug rings on a table in a funeral parlour are what Myfanwy once called infra dig. She is a clever lady and the light of my life and good at French, see?. I heard tell that some people and I expect mostly abroad have sofas and even a small snack room but that seems to me a shade too, what is it, *decorous* for the occasion. *Cake is for the wake*. Myfanwy, is that what you said, my love? And you're not wanting the parlour to look like a Little Chef.'

Came a voice: 'Yes, Evans. Tea and remember the sugar and milk but small biscuits on a nice plate is not going too far. With doilies for a homely touch.'

'Now, have you thought about the hearse and the lead car? That'll be tens of thousands of pounds boy. But you can lease. I will see what I can find out for up your way. And bargain, boy, *bargain*. There is no shame, but you don't do it like you are common. And get a discount on the insurance, *now te*. Tell the business fellows you'll provide for them in their demise, tidy-like. And there's general liability insurance. You remember all this from college, yes? Two kinds, write them down and bargain like a professional, boy. Two kinds of insurance, yes? And don't confuse them. Not as though you can insure against death, is it? Even with the faith. Myfanwy's husband and brother and so all praying to the Virgin and your sister Perfection, too and that was not insurance, now was it, lad?' And there came a voice that was rather more booming than muffled:

'Evans the Bodies! That is irreligious and no way to be speaking, even though you are my true love.'

Slowly slowly we put the business together, Ned and I, though the demands of the locals were harsh. They wanted green burials and we couldn't cater; cardboard coffins which embarrassed me; wouldn't stand for anything other than natural materials in the caskets while we loved the crackle of polyester as I had had with Evans. And some of them thought we were common, I expect, but we did our best. Halls decked out like the Taj Mahal; churches without proper singing: I mean without the boom and clarion call of the Welsh voice. There was a reverberation missing in the polite caroling and I realised I was homesick to the core and heartsick for Seren who, though sour, was the most beautiful thing in the world to me. We laboured on, though. We had premises, all proper, and everything as Evans the Bodies had recommended.

But all this time I was emptier than the awaiting coffins.

One day, Ned came in, heartsick, too. He had Anna-Katrina, of course, and she loved the boy, though the boy's mother wanted a headland girl; one who would understand. But that is not what I want to tell you, now. Ned came in, empty. He had assisted at the funeral of Mrs Ann Smithers, who had died of drink from the sadness. Neighbours were always shovelling her off the path, where she lay paralytic, though she was in her seventies now, and should have been cared for. She was found, day over, prone in the bed, radio on and cat squealing.

Find me; feed me: *help me*. Like my twilight by the sea cave.

She wasn't smiling because she died alone. And she wasn't smiling because she was sick with the drink. And this lady, funny, ebullient and brilliant, lived all over and never lost home, like I did, well she drank because she had loved another woman and been disowned by her disgusted family, then she had found, she thought, love. Ah, but the woman ran to a husband she did not love and to her own disgusted family who forgave her and Ann rocked shut and was ashamed and the sadness, in the end, took over. And no-one came. Until one day, late in the drink days, came cousins from away and, when she died, they got everything and we all watched them throw her things into the skip and clutch the winnings and, worst, present a funeral of their own contriving, which was not her.

She sang, Ann, and read poetry; once I sat with her myself and we gorged ourselves on the words in candlelight. Once, for us, understanding like a *Cymraeg* the heartsickness and the *hiraeth*, she read Dylan Thomas's *A Child's Christmas in Wales* when the season was coming and we were bathed in Advent and she tried to do Mrs Prothero and Miss Prothero and her accent was hopeless, but we laughed, laughed, laughed and oh, the room was a world of love, see? But at her funeral, it was a dry season and there was, the cousins said, to be no music and no poetry and no singing, just a brief send off down the track-like, and then sandwiches but you had to buy your own drinks and there was not even a cup of tea. And Ned grieved for her, walking past the skip they put her life in: past jewellery and book junk they didn't understand was treasure—and old maps and secrets and a life. And everyone saw but nobody did anything and Ned mourned because he too said nothing, though he felt everything in his heart. She could not be who she was; perfect, whole. In death, even. And the sex? *Why, why, for why*, should it matter? As I said, I am telling you more than one story here. Death in life and life in death, but I also told you of Ned giving me the eye when we were younger. We are fluid, protean, girl: like angels, unconfined. And I said to Ned, 'Maybe we cannot stay here?' and the boy cried and he was in my arms and there we are, see.

Then Ned told me a story of himself; of Anna-Katrina. He

loved her, but home *more*, he thought. He told me he had half heard things of the history of Miss Davies and Clandestine House and had waited to say because what he had half heard was surely at least a quarter wrong. And then our Rhys came to visit and oh, I had missed him but I was ashamed of his rough ways and what he could not do in company; the small talk and tidy chat they expected around here and I was ashamed of my shame. He brought news that Seren was again at Clandestine House if I should want to see her and I saw that he had known, all along, of my love for the sour, suffering beauty and I cried to know what else there was to know, so Rhys told me of Miss Davies's romantic disappointment and how it is had consumed her and the fine, crumbling house all around her. The radiant bride on her wedding day, left alone by her man—for then the hands turning into old claws and the back bent like the frame of a coracle with the abandonment; the penumbra of the beautiful house; the outcast world and the witchery that came from out and within; the house with its pictures changed so as never to experience the real people of the world, all around, at night and in morning quiet moments when you look at your Dear Dears on the wall and say, 'Good morning Mammy. Goodnight Bronwen or good afternoon, Eleri' or whatever hers were called. And no baby for her, as for poor Perfection, but a child, sweet, pretty little girl come to live there with the well-off spinster on the Cleddau and trained up to remember the words I had heard and which my girls, in their landforms, had heard: 'Break their hearts.' And I understood, though inchoately girl, that the respiring house and the creeping mud and the moss that moved were made by the deepest unhappiness you could feel, but also by something else, of nature upturned and perverted and foul as fair and fair as foul and something all to do with Seren and with Daddy, but I did not know what or how. I thought that I could know if I discovered where she had come from and find the Story of a Star. And as for Ned, he would come with me, help me, when he could. But for now, he must cry and stay here, run the business, like. Rhys said, 'Let's go home, boy?' And the phone rang. Morgan the Pints.

Perfection was dead.

She had waited until I was settled as she thought, and Rhys was with me, so as not to find her. They found her out there. With every last impulse in that body and straining across her anagram of a good face, she dragged herself down and over. They found her out there, but the mystery was how she got so far as the sea cave and was smiling and warm.

Stories to tell, isn't it?

Love is not circular or linear or logical and as I say, I am telling you more than one story.

10

The story of a star

You know, it hurts, doesn't it, that in duty of care there may be misprision? Once, Perfection, ugly and shunned by our beautiful mother, was aware of Mammy walking out, round St Brides Bay, with a pretty fair-haired girl from the village. A distant cousin, somehow. Afterwards, I said to my sister that Pretty was a spare room, bunk-up child of someone after evenings at The Sloop. That was not nice of me, I know. But when my brutal sister grieved, well then I was *wicked* for it. *Wicked* in my longed defence of her. Then again and again. Pretty, Pretty, Pretty, rounding the headland, deep in conversation and all. Talking, talking; laughing and tossing hair and all coquette with Pretty. Perfection saw it: 'Why not me, Mammy?' I heard her crying.

'You remind me too much of him.'

I thought, at first, that she meant me. Now I see she meant my father, who was misplaced. But I was telling you of my sister. That time, I went into her room, and touched her shoulder in love; later, she pushed this to me: a poem? From Perfection?

'This time I am keeping a record. It is my pain, Almost. And I promise not to tear up your record. I did wrong. Here: look, see: this is Pretty. And I am cariad, but not really dear: spat at; brought up brutal while Mammy beams at the fair-haired girl: metre all over the place, is it? Still, here:

Rounding the headland at St Brides and sighting the small churchyard,
cariad, you were aware, weren't you now, that things were changed that day?
You saw us with the girl, cousin by marriage, I think she was,
and all was well because she was not you. You were, weren't you now,
the same age and the same beauty and the same dimension, even, roughly now,
and all so different because she was not you. And Daddy said, I know he did,
Ah, my lovely girl, my cariad, look at your lovely golden hair
and your blue eyes and the light foot and a tumble of a laugh—
but that was not for you, but for your cousin, by marriage I think she was,
and she was fair and pretty and you with your welter of a laugh
and your thin voice and your pinched nose and you my shameless,

shameful little girl, mine but not mine and yapping now
as we rounded the headland at St Brides. Sing to the sailors, girl,
cry for the mermaids if you see them there, but in this dark world
where cliffs heap up and the boy drowns and the wrack fills,
think always that none of this cares for you, but for her, cariad.

'*I* care for you, Perfection. I always will.'

Then we both sobbed and, oh, we howled! 'Why does no-one love us. But us? And even so we do it wrong, like!'

And my sister was gone now, on the rocks, somehow. And so Rhys and I went to her, Ned left heartsick but efficient with the Dead Dears of Wiltshire, for the time being, and in bed, afternoons, with Anna-Katrina. That bed which was sometimes ours. Keep a broad mind, girl. More things there should be, in our philosophy. Bed; time; family; things of heart-stopping beauty. Being dead. And also not. But as I was saying…

The smaller road to the bigger road runs in windings through the deep woods; named for an old witch called Sally, then straight lines to Pennsylvania and the no-trees in a very straight line that worried me, always. Then it is like this, as I told you before, but backwards. In Haverfordwest, there are many roundabouts and a myriad cars and a stone circle almost absorbed into a supermarket car park, then, as you go further, Narberth and Llanddewi Velfrey, where ancient uncles of mine, as Mammy used to say, kept their women, and a strange blind aunt fixed you with her cruel eye and you could not move from the spot as she rooted you like she had the power of a Preseli gorgon and underneath her cap were snakes; then you see that part of the Pembrokeshire National Park which they sold off, though they said they never would, to make a posh holiday resort mostly for the people from away and on this place, covered with little villas and facilities, stands the old Newton farm where my grandmother, Bronwen, was born. I expect she haunts them now, all the shrieking swimmers, piercing their feet like a weever fish as they swirl unselfconsciously through the unreal water. With her ill-fitting teeth that go clackety-clack and she won't have them fixed because it's vanity. And you see the purple mountains and out there near Nevern of The Bleeding Yew Tree, is Pentre Ifan, the dolmen where my father used to go and think, it was said, before he was misplaced and then you are in Carmarthen, all stripped out at its heart by the new developments where my family used to bet and smoke pipes and walk down to the cattle market and my long-gone and whiskered matriarchs out-bid any men with both money and spirit.

These places are made new, but they are all haunted. In the new builds at night, ancient dead people spit and stir and their very atoms unsettle the casual drinker in the pub or walker to the fancy hotels and tea rooms and places that do up old crafts and sell them as vintage. And you drive on and reach the big motorway and you glimpse Cardiff Bay and then I hoped my girls were bobbing out there beyond Steep Holm and Flat

Holm islands and laughing. So on towards the sweeps of the Severn and the mud and the ammonites in its cliffs at Aust and their dangerous, terrible tides and oh, the bridge is like a soft green galleon, with its curves and sweeps of railing and wires like sails and it turns sensuously and then you land and it says *Croeso i Gymru* and your heart goes thump into your shoes and it is over and you're happy and you fancy yourself back just across the sweep of the river and then you are at home.

So, Rhys and I swept up a valley, past the line of tall trees you can see from anywhere, and down another valley, through that place called Pennsylvania although I saw no woods there, just an angry narrow road bisecting a once-village, and away to your side had been the city in the bowl and it was fine, alright, but was too alive and not haunted enough or properly so and it had been varnished and sanded. And oh! I had tried. Then, the grateful orbit down to sea and the bitter, glorious punch and teeth of the headland and Thank God, *Croeso i Gymru*, wanting to be grand, and we are there, *we are there*. Pembrokeshire; *Sir Benfro*. I realised I was speaking aloud, narrating like Evans the Bodies and 'Shut up, shut up' said Rhys and then we were both howling and scratching at our limbs with the relief of being home and the pain of Perfection that was destroyed, silent, lost and that by her own hand.

So, Charity House.

They had brought her up, cooling now, calm, from the sea cave and she was lying in our front room and there was Gwyneth by her side, lovingly pressing her hair back. And I saw Rhys press Gwyneth's hand and I knew why Perfection had done a kind thing and that, one day, Rhys and Gwyneth, would have a baby, perfect like the alabaster pebble, that was beyond Perfection and it was very wrong, but right. And Dr Morgan the Pints had pronounced as well as he could; then later Evans the Bodies came, thus with him Myfanwy and they, so cognisant of death, held us all and Evans he said, 'Now, te. It is better like this. She was a strange one when we cared for her out at the parlour. Never a sigh, just peaceful and look, Almost, she is not an anagram anymore but all in the right place and lovely, ah look at her Cariad with a capital C and, look you, as pretty as the Virgin Mary'.

Then Muffled Myfanwy, who spoke and spoke and sang like a lark, now I had had released her pretty voice, she said, 'Evans, there's a soft man you are but a good one. Now let us care for this poor girl' and I thought, 'How did Evans know I said Perfection had an anagram of a good face?' I'd forgotten, a moment, that around here, thoughts carry.

Thoughts carry.

I, to my old room while they cried and smiled and Perfection lay.

Thoughts carry.

Now: I heard it across the room. The sea was infiltrating it. The ceiling white to pale blue; iridescence, then navy. Sea change; something rich and strange.

Derian, from a long way away, telling me he was helping and he was less sad now.

Derian, from a long way away, telling me that he was of this

world but something more, and not always in land dress.
Derian telling me that he was clothed as he should be.
Derian all mixed up—and for why?—with the voices of my girls, Nerys and Dilys.
Seren. Dressed not as she should be.
With Derian, without him.
Seren, looking for her clothing.
Not clothed as she should be,
Lying on a gravestone at Capel Dewi, out at Walton West as the sea whipped.
Crying for one another—
Found and lost:
Williams;
Volpone, taking her up and casting her down, a cheap thing.
Far away, at sea, inland,
Clandestine House and the claw handed spinster, whom I loved—
Then again, Derian, and the blurring of my edges: he shone, I saw it then, I'd seen it before and thought it only the moonlight—

Now I felt the indistinctness of my edges and a rage rising up. The man who took Perfection, who beat her and silenced her. He was known to me, in my heart, though misplaced, and now out of my heart: *he took them all*. Eleri, Bronwen, Mammy, Perfection. *He was not misplaced*; he was very much there and bloody and livid and scything because he hated the world; my voice rose up and I felt the hand of Derian brushing my arm who was scintillating and of the sea-way, not the land-ways and off a coast, in some other part of the country, my father put his pots down over the edge of his fine boat and laughed at his work complete, thinking of a new girl, with hot limbs, but then I rose up in the boat with him, in all strength: thoughts travel. Daddy was pushed down, under, below, and there, with him, pulling deeper, were my girls and the tough hands of the mermen, too: thoughts carry. Down under the pots, they knew what he was too: the pincers bit his face and the creatures came in early and his face was barnacled and he was not misplaced but set where he should be, under the water, too deep and sanded-in to come up.

The girls rose up, from a different sea: I could feel them in my hot blood.

The misanthrope, debtor, murderer, traitor, clogged under the soft sand—

And I thought I heard Perfection sigh, then.

So, she was laid to rest, now. And we buried my sister at Capel Dewi and I knew it was time to visit Miss Davies to know of Seren; to know more. I would compel her to tell me as I compelled my father to drown. Now he was placed, not misplaced, and could not hurt. Evans would have said that there was an hour for repentance and thus the hereafter, but I was not sure. And then in my veins coursed the love and scorn of Mammy, of Bronwen and Eleri, alive in death and buzzing in my blood. The name Mammy had given me, as a taunt, I thought. Was it possible that I had misunderstood it? I heard their voices; clear as day; as sea-light.

Eleri: 'Go to her, boy.'

Bronwen: 'Reach her, lad.'

Mammy: 'Find her, release her, son.'

Perfection: 'It is love indeed brother, and it was always stronger than the hate.'

And from the silt, Daddy tried to speak and in a carmine flurry in my mind, he was silenced still worse by the women and by my girls, down, down. In sand, forever entombed.

Miss Davies, chuffing like an old train, answered the door of Clandestine House; I felt the broom and rosemary at the door scrape across my feet more coarsely than usual and there was a rustle to one side, the tang of salt drops: Nerys and Dilys had swum like a flash up the Cleddau and now took land forms to watch me safe. Spinster claws of the old woman grasped, but there was love here in bent backs and sad cataracts. There was love in the webbed eyes and sad gait, I knew. Somewhere at the back of the house I sensed Seren waited, exhausted by I knew not what.

I could not have made conversation; the time of day; the quality of the air. It could only be all her, all star, and in a rush. So:

'I love her, Miss Davies. She is indivisible from me, I will always love her. She does not say it, only flares with spite, but I see it in her, too. She is part of my existence, part of myself. She has been in every line I have ever read, since I first came to Clandestine House, the rough common headland boy who played among the Dead Dears at Capel Dewi, and whose poor heart she wounded even then. She has been in every prospect I have ever seen since—on the streams across Nolton and the bay mouth, the drowning cove and blue lagoon; on the sails of the ships, on the coastal walks, the cree of the curlews, the foot-creeping moss; in the clouds, in the light, in the darkness, in the wind, in the woods on the Cleddau, the lily-ponds at Bosherston, the glorious bite of the sea down to Barafundle, in the streets; the embodiment of every graceful fancy that my mind has ever become acquainted with. The coffin hatch at my house, the brimming lights of the headland, the sulphur stones of Bath and the tidy stones of which the strongest London buildings are made, are not more real, or more impossible to be displaced by her hands, than her presence and influence have been to me, there and everywhere, and will be. Seren, star, to the last hour of my life, she cannot choose, Miss Davies, but remain part of my character, part of the little good in me, part of the evil. I associate her, cruel, sullen and scornful, only with the good, and I will faithfully hold her to that always, for even so she must have done me far more good than harm, let me feel now what sharp distress I may. Star!

O God bless her, God forgive her for her cruelty! God help to cure her pain. Miss Davies, God help to cure yours and I think that my own hands can help too: the blurring at my edges, the sea cave. I am different now, I know it. Derian Llewhellin!' (She started at the name.) '*Tell me*. Why should Seren break hearts? Why is her own heart broken that she should hate the world so? And tell me now: where did she came from? *For why* is she yours? And while I am here, caught up in this anger and grief, I want to know what you can tell me about the money given to me? It isn't yours, though I always thought it would be, but whose is it?'

Miss Davies sat heavily as I compelled her and began. 'Very well, boy.' She was crying.

'The child was found out at Capel Dewi, curled like a fern frond on a Llewhellin grave, shivering and half asleep. She belonged to no-one and she was terribly strange. The priest found her and she was clutching and scratching at her legs, unable first to walk. Williams—you met him of course—was here then. I doubt he mentioned he used to live here, a Cymraeg casting off. He saw us as animals; rough beasts slouching we were and his law didn't work here because we saw through his pride. He was once a Welshman, you know, hating who he was, changing his voice, going rotten as he bested the Severn and longed for the Home Counties. But some thought him impressive and he was called, lifting the child like a dirty blot I bet, bach, and bringing it to the rich mad lady who could provide. I am sorry I did not tell you of knowing him. Once, when I was young and callow, I too thought him impressive, flirted with him; he took my hand and swarmed scorn on me. Always scorn for me. So lonely. And I had longed for a child; I had said it. But then, again, I was wronged: cheated and left on my wedding day by another man: all for money. I cannot speak his name. Then I lost all faith in the world, but my hatred, boy, animated the world around and the moss crept and the cree of the curlew was louder and that wrack against the harbour wall at Clandestine, well now, it *crept* alive, beached up, because of my hate. He broke my heart. My wedding day. Every day I make my house anew, never at rest. But I am more like you than you think Almost. Thoughts carry and your father is gone.'

'You knew?'

'I *felt* it, Almost.'

'I want to know but tell me first of Seren.'

'Yes the sweet little child. Williams came to Clandestine and dropped her from his hands like a distasteful canker, a blot and I took her.'

'But how could you take her in? She was someone's child! She must have been.'

'Don't you *feel* it Almost? She is not of our world. She is a child of the sea. She is a mermaid girl who could not go home. A mermaid child who took land garb to see a pretty boy she glimpsed in a sea cave and wandered too far and lost her sea dress. Remember, Almost: you *know* this, don't you? If the garb be lost, the hapless being must unavoidably become an inhabitant of the earth.'

'And the boy…'

Then I knew.

It was me, sand child slipping out from a sad house to the sea cave, years away from Christmas Eve and Derian Llewhellin. The voice I heard on the beach; the voices I had always known. *Her*; her family out there calling to her; to me. My eyes welled up, for her.

'She will always love you, but she has never had one hour's

happiness in your society because, boy, it was for you, sweet one, that a little girl came on land and wandered and was lost and yet her mind all day, all night, is harping on the happiness of having her with you until death. It is a terrible paradox. Your love for her is pain, too, is it not? I do not know if a time between you will be possible. I know that, in my loathing of the world, my dusty house and broken heart, I have taught her only terrible things, all compacted up with the loss of her own, her proper body, her life. She has been a vassal to fill and it is something I can never forgive myself for. But Seren. Come out here now, he is here. And I was wrong!'

The old woman railed and beat her chest with her claw hand and oh, it was dreadful to see what was occurring. And then, and then, I thought just for a moment… but will she? Seren: will she come out. Too late yet? And I was held in that skein of time and waited.

But a girl squalled and banged a door and howled in rage and would not see me. And Miss Davies, broken more, wept in my arms and howled, 'Almost: you have it in you. I feel it. Of this place like you, where thoughts carry and, when young, our edges blur if we fulfil our birthright or when the right hand brushes our arm and gives us power that is extraordinary if only we learn to use it. Almost, you have it in you. Make love stronger than hate or make them settle, metaphysical, like, the burning tree and the green leaf all in one. *Make it happen* Almost.'

11

She burns

My mother taught at Wiston school,
her hands were lithe, her mind so sharp,
her friend Rhiannon worshipped her
And plucked her name upon the harp
Which sat all gold, in sight of all,
Rhiannon's talons told mother's fall—
a pizzicato death through strings,
her cruel nails scratched their goal:
Your mother will have feet, not wings
and with their clay, they'll crush her soul—
Oh read *The Mabinogi*, dear,
you pretty pretty little child—
for you shall be my daughter fair,
my son Avaggdu's ugly—wild—
the thick and thwart upon his brow
why should she have while I've not got?

Your mother taught at Wiston school
and so I tell you, she shall not.
She plucked and plucked and screamed her rage
now Mother's clad in primrose dell,
but I can't go and see her now,
Rhiannon keeps me in a cage
and sings to me of sweetest love
and all the things I cannot tell:
Avaddgu cries for he's not loved,
and spits upon upon sweet mother's grave.

This is an old poem that I read once; of its provenance I was unsure, but I think it was a curse upon my mother, upon Mammy; I found a copy of it with her things when she had gone. I knew that Mammy had had a friend on the mountain called Rhiannon, a harpist, But if it was true and not an experiment, then who were the children in it? Round here, where thoughts carry, could it have been me, crushed by life and Mammy with feet of clay? But I had a notion of my terrible, wonderful mother being at peace and then, that night I met Derian Llewhellin, well now, his quiet fingers had brushed off on my sleeve some compelling power; he had chosen to divest some of his strength I thought. And it was not just strength, but magic. But why and how should he have it? Or I?

The next day, I went to see Miss Davies again.

It was as if the house were opening up to me, allowing me in, in birth pangs or death throes, I could not say.

I walked through rooms I had never seen before.

That weeping house showed me chambers that I had never known before.

Antimacassars; tortured drapes; rooms held up by dust and regret.

Daybeds, with books left open upon them, breaking along their spines.

Then the old dining room, worse than the place where we had our fine Christmas dinners; penumbras from the crystal lights more oily and nasty.

Tapers and a blazing fire.

There on a long oak table, sable with dust, stood a confection. At first I did not understand it to be so; its turns and whorls were almost lovely by candlelight, but as I approached, the sour-sweet smell assailed, worse than in the milking parlour of Evans the Bodies. (Although we were inured to that.) From this chamber, the daylight was completely excluded, and it had an airless smell that was oppressive. Smoke hung in the room and felt colder than the winter air—like the mist whirling round the sea cave or the obscuring of our Capel Dewi at unbidden times of day; off the sea ways, but oh not fresh like that. The tall candles troubled and worried its darkness and it was a large room, big as I imagined an old ballroom might be, but every discernible thing in it was covered with dust and mould, and dropping to pieces. On the long table, almost like an unclean altar, was the strange centrepiece and in the room beyond were dusty pictures which looked as if they had been set—as they were, and not changed by their mistress like those in the rest of the house, and the clocks were all stopped at two o'clock. When, I thought, the house and the clocks and the hearts stopped all together. And why did her heart contract at that unholy hour? And as I looked along the sable dust covering, I saw that the confection was a black and yellow tower, shrouded with the oily penumbra, like an odious black fungus, and it was teeming and alive; I saw speckle-legged spiders with blotchy bodies run home to it, and running out from it, and from elsewhere I heard sobs.

'Depredation, Almost. It; me; my body; my home; my heart; my ghastly wedding feast, just as it was. Two o'clock. My heart… my heart it contracted at that unholy hour! The time of my marriage!' Miss Davies entered the room. 'And now you see all, boy.' She shook and wailed and there was nothing I could do, I thought. She wailed, 'Seren, it is too late. Roland Griffiths, he took her. He is a lump of a man. He is a rich, sulky beast, but she decided she could trap him so she did. Then he asked and she agreed. She has gone to live in his gilded cage. But she cannot break his heart, for there is no heart to break!'

Roland Griffiths, inheritor of the land around the quay and owner of several farms. A hulk of a stone man, who rarely spoke because his money did that for him. Doubtless he would have admired the ways of Williams with his Volpone and his Temple. You could see Griffiths sometimes, mean Atlas, everything around here that was green and had hope bulbing on his shoulders. He was a man to loathe; an empty man who succeeded, in this life, in getting what he wanted.

Now, the most beautiful girl under the heavens. I had thought my own heart was broken before; now I *knew* it was.

I cried from the ground under my feet, up, up, up and Miss Davies wept, too: 'More, Almost!' and I wept back that I could not take it all in and yet she told me:

'Derian, Almost. The convict, criminal as they saw him! He sent you the money! He is in hiding but rich beyond our dreams through some schemes he has and honourable schemes too. Williams told me, when he came to visit his Dead Dears though I was to keep it quiet. That he should care at all and that the criminal should have succeeded in this way. Every year Williams comes to the quay; he was my friend, once! Now he comes to spit and stare at me; at us; at the night world of the quay—the moss that creeps, the wrack that thrusts itself up the shingle, boy; he hates it and comes to scorn it. I made him tell me. He was Derian's friend once, too, as a boy. They played out at Capel Dewi, ran the coast paths and flew their clumsy kites on the headland. Derian came to him: "The boy saved me and he is special," said he.

'Williams did not understand what that meant: to save someone else or to be special. But I knew. That you had it in you before and that he had given you more. You felt it, didn't you? A softening at your edges? Your form becoming indeterminate: sea change! Out at the cave!'

She had more to say, but before I could stop her, pain and rage caught her up too badly: Miss Davies ran at the table and at the tapers. The flame caught the musty and billowing black skirts in which she swam and she was set on fire. Up she went, dry and delicate; clawed hands clutching at the air: 'Forgive me Almost! Forgive yourself. Forgive that man I loved for he has been taken by the sea!'

I rolled her in drapes, I saved her momentarily and I hurt myself. You know my scars. She was dying, crying of how she treated Seren and of her manipulation and bad deeds and yet… her clawed hands clutched at my back, as they always did, but then they loosened and she seemed… she seemed to become airier, then less dry; to begin a movement, a transmigration, to sail away.

'Take me to the quay. Release me, Almost. Say I drowned.'

Lighter and lighter her body still. I called for my girls, and they came, in a flash, Nerys and Dilys, and they smiled and kissed my crone and took her under the water and said,

'She is at rest, now, Almost. And look what we have. What we found, led to it by the willow at Clandestine. It is garb!'

And with this they touched her and clothed her, colour now; black cowls not more—then Miss Davies took a sea breath and died to the land world and she was lost and found and whispering the name that before she could not bear to mouth: the man who left her on her wedding day—'Tell me Miss Davies!'—but then I saw she was at peace and understood that she was mermaid, like Seren, trapped in the world, blasted into sorrow on her wedding day and her sea garb taken by her husband to be, so he could possess her, though he cast her out. And I thought, you see, that again I wanted to know. She didn't tell me. I hadn't asked her. I was burned up with love for her and surprise at my glorious chanting girls. I didn't know who broke her heart. But I would find out, because now I knew I could.

Round here: thoughts travel.
And, around here, the trees suck air and, at night,
when the last shriek of the plump and pretty-breasted curlew
is drawn from its throat, and when the strand-line treasure
is dulled and shredded against the rock, even in fair weather,
well then: that is the time to take our fill.
Oh yes.
Around here, when the moss
spawns bad, it creeps across your foot if you slowly move,
so be sure to move quite fast, when the twilight stalks,
then that is the time when we take our fill.
You remember this? From earlier, like?

On Christmas eve, as the sea whipped, I met Derian Llewhellin and he, like me, was on the run. 'We are all on the run from something boy, oh yes, oh yes,' he told me. And then that man brushed my arm with his fingertips and I was sea changed. I felt a little more of what it is to interpret the sea and the land and to move with them, animate through them, but I couldn't articulate it yet. I was learning, though. For then, in the soft evening breeze, the arm of a willow brushed my sleeve; its green circling my fingers so that I was compelled to turn toward its trunk. There, carved into his soft heart, just discernible, was another heart: its legend said 'AD and AL.' I knew: Aeres Davies (that was Miss Davies and her name meant *heiress* in our tongue) and I saw who the other was: Arwyn Llewhellin (who was my father). She had told me, then: the world of the quay carried on her language and said that it was my own Daddy—who was misplaced then buried under the silt—who had left her on her wedding day.

12

Turn of the tide

That old man, the schoolteacher, dead in a mound of violets and, so Derian told me at the sea cave, presumed at his hand, well now I had always been a bit scared of him. I remember being made to talk to him as a small child and when I truanted, to learn in the lanes and the headland, on my own, I would meet him and he looked at me keenly through his rheumy eyes. Always old; he didn't curse me or blast me for skipping the work to which he had devoted his life. We looked at each other and it took me a long time to understand his acceptance of me and that I loved him. Memories of beautiful Mammy, Eleri and Bronwen, when alive, burned my fingers. I looked at my mother and her beauty was seared into me; scorn too, I thought at the time. But the thing is, now, that even those we curse or who bore us; whose weak constitution frustrates us as we stride out on the sea cliff, we miss them, girl. The love: not circular, linear or logical.

Such it was with Old Llewhellin. I was trying to put it in words; since Perfection died, I was putting everything down in words.

Ah,
I had longed not to talk to him, the schoolmaster;
He was always old, even as a boy, Llewhelli
His eyes blorted thick, his voice rasped:
Never a pretty thing was he.
But I misses him now, you see, that old man
Cresting the corners of the foxgloved lanes—
Standing by the sea-view graves at the tankers
Bound for Milford from great bright places
He hadn't seen and didn't want.
And I misses the silent pouring of tea
And the picking of apples from his headland-wizened trees;
the storied estuary, century feuds and nodding campion.
And I cry when I scent, alone, the violet patch, dug up,
Where I found him. And he was gone, eyes closed and young.

And now I was so sad. I wrote to Ned and asked him, when he could, to write to me and said that I would be back soon to help him run the business, although I did not know how I would tear myself away from here and the revelations that came thick and fast. I wrote, 'My heart is broken' and Ned wrote—I heard it—'I knows it' and his Pembrokeshire grammar had forgotten to go posh that time and the boy needed me in his bed, though he had his Anna-Katrina.

I was back at Charity House with Rhys. Gwyneth stayed on to help him, her pretty chatter a comfort to him and to us. There was kind chatter and a soft bed for them, too. There came a letter: *Almost Llewhellin* and it was on stiff formal paper and stamped on its back, HM Prison, Swansea. I opened it:

Oystermouth Road,
Sandfields,
Swansea.

Dear Boy. Are you nearly there, is it?

It was from Derian Llewhellin.

I'm sorry for my silly jokes, boy, but here I am, at her Majesty's Leisure and with a little job, too! But I am incarcerated. I am told I have lived a life of crime; my trial for your uncle found dead in a bed of violets is yet to come, but there have been other bad things. I have fought and hurt and raged and, Almost, it was all because I have loved and lost and I am not a land man. Here, they sty me up, boy. Make me talk to people; suggest, and they are kind, with it, that my reality is curated and my personality at best borderline or that I have a fanciful notion of who or what I am. I will confide in you boy because I understand that you will understand and I have things to tell you and I want you to keep them to your heart and to come to see me if you can. I say my trial for your uncle found dead in a bed of violets is yet to come, but I am sick, Almost. Can you see by my hand?' (I could; oh, I could.) *'You know, don't you, that when I brushed your hand, just a touch now, at the sea cave on*

Christmas Eve, that you were changed? I am tired now, but you are just beginning. I pass things to you. Stories; power; ever-moving. Please come and see me. You will be allowed. I am sorry, boy that we did not have more time. There are reasons that you mean so much to me; I feel I knew you before you remember and before I remember and I knew your father before he was misplaced and he, Almost, was a bad man and you deserved so much more. I wish we had met in better circumstances. I wish that I could have been your second father and you, my son—more to me than any son and with my daughter, too. I will tell you the rest. Come as soon as you can.

Of course. Second father and you my son.

It was not so far, where Derian waited; up from Haverfordwest by train and in the direction of Ned and our other home; our other dead, beyond the Bristol Channel and abroad. On Oystermouth Road I could feel the sea light on my back and know that, behind me, out and out, the gulls circled. If I went further, well up from here it is such a sweep of coast, Llanelli way, a white light follows you with the broad shallow sweeps of sea and up at Burry Port there is an extraordinary signpost: New York, Trepassey, Paris, London: the modest yellow brick monument to Amelia Earhart, who had touched down here, rather than Ireland or Southampton in the flight before the one where she was lost forever. I saw that sign once; felt the pull of those places and then a man behind me, all sour, said, telling the story as we do (and that is what a Cymraeg does best; well, one of the things),

'Typical of Burry Port to claim all the glory, is it? My

uncle, you see, he saw her get out of her plane. She couldn't understand us and my uncle, he shouted, "You're in Pwll Slip" and she slammed the door of her seaplane and I don't think there's ever an excuse for that sort of rudeness, even if your plane comes down, now is it? But that monument: it belongs to Pwll.'

And I said, 'Quite, Sir. Never an excuse for rudeness.'

'Even at your own funeral. Even when you're dead. And being drowned, like.'

I was remembering, as I went, these storied places, up and down this coast, Pembrokeshire, Carmarthenshire. The sign outside Kidwelly telling you to slow down because the otters were crossing; a story Eleri once told me about shipping off to Caldey Island from Tenby with a mute oarsman and a lady with a clubfoot; and they looked and looked at each other, mute and club foot, and on the island, went off, clunking, gesticulating and Eleri had to find a new oarsmen because the monks were closing up and the lovers gone to ground in the clerestory. It's these stories that are life blood. Love in a funeral parlour; Evans and Myfanwy, I, after Derian Llewhellin, giving a moth breath, now.

Did you sigh there? You're thinking, *Tell me about Derian, in Swansea, Almost.* Well yes, yes. I am telling you more than one story. That is said before, girl! Well now, up the coast road was the prison, and I met a warder who once knew me as a baby and Bronwen and Eleri and who lip curled at the words, 'Your daddy' (I did not ask about that meeting; I was getting further measure of a history and knew I would find out more) and I went to him, Derian, amid the laundry smell and wash of disinfectant. Behind me, the sun hung low and there he was, stretched out on his bed, with a dancing magic filming over in those eyes.

'Oh dear boy,' he wept to me, 'whatever happens and however I go. I'm quite content to take my chance with it, land or sea. I've seen you boy, and you can be a fine young man without me. The money I made, all yours. It is honest money, I've made arrangements that if they found me guilty it would not be seized by the crown. And the other things, oh Almost, the night we met at the sea cave! I was running but I knew you would be there, though I pretended not to know you for it was too painful!'

I sat down heavily. Grey blankets, metal bed, white sink. Here, in 1958, in Swansea prison, the last man to be hanged in Wales was dispatched. He killed a postmaster and when that last man went to the safe, so found it locked and ran empty handed from Fforestfach. I shuddered, as I recalled. And now, it was all too real, colliding with this Derian who was preternatural and rare, but then I remembered this was how it was: the green-leaved, burning tree of *The Mabinogi*; the contrary passions side by side: the disparate seasons in one mood, one breath:

'Oh Derian, tell me who you are, what you are and who I am? I will never stir from your side,' said I: 'I will be true to you' and wept with my heart breaking again and behind my eyes was Seren because there was always Seren.

'I see her boy. I see her in you.'

I felt his hand tremble as it held mine, and he turned his face away as he lay on the metal bed and I so hoped that I would not disappoint him now that he had enriched me and I wanted to know. I did know. All of a sudden.

'*Seren. She is yours*, isn't she and you—?'

'Yes, she is my daughter. Like her, I am of the sea. She came to answer the call of the boy she loved from birth and I felt it in my bones that this was you. I went to find you out there. Sometimes, because I am a reckless man and unsettled, I took my land form and came on the sand and into the towns and I made mischief and I quarrelled. It was an adventure I could not resist. I am not so good as the rest of my kind, although mermaids, as you know, will stifle and bury under the sand, if they must and as you bid them.'

'Dilys and Nerys…'

'Yes, known to me in all their glory. And you, boy, will know just what I mean by that. I see you blush. Don't be ashamed, boy. This is the natural way of things. Bed; life; death and, most of all, love.'

'Oh, Derian.' I was crying now, see.

'I came, once, with my sea garb in my safe-bag, to Little Haven and The Sloop and I met a rough man who came over, all conspiratorial-like, and that was your father. I had a sea look; briny: he thought me a kindred spirit and over pints I compelled him to tell me of the things he had done. That he had wooed the spinster at Clandestine House and she, Almost, was kind to me and I to her. She did not know I was Seren's father. For when your daddy left her on their wedding day and before he treated your mother so badly, well now I felt for this poor lady, bent backed and new-old with her clawed hands and those dreadful tapers and the shutters up. And she felt for me, thinking me some sort of wanderer, or outcast. And so when she found the little girl, my daughter, out at Capel Dewi and her garb all lost and nothing I could do then… I am faltering to tell you boy… well now, I kept my silence because that little girl, she was lost to the sea, though she felt its ache, and the lady loved her. I saw, as she got older that Seren, as you call her, was following the sour life of her mother-mistress, but by then there was little I could do. I kept coming back, though, boy. She was my little girl and she came on land for you, for the little boy she loved and hated because, through love of him, she had discarded her garb.'

Derian raised his hand, tears in his eyes: 'No, boy, I do not blame you. And boy, your father, it was your father who shocked and pushed old Llewhellin the schoolmaster into the bed of violets, for spite of the old man's watchful joy; because he hated the joy and the love. But then he was never there and always misplaced. I had followed him to that house, because I was watchful of him; watchful of you and over my girl. I have always watched you, like you were my son and more to me than any son, and I hoped against hope that you were for my mermaid-child.'

It was too much. I broke and I railed.

'Quiet boy, we must be quiet. It is lucky that I am sick enough for you to see me here and not in the cell. There are many crimes lined up for me and all for being in the wrong place at the wrong time while your own father committed them.'

Time stood still on Oystermouth Road. At Clandestine House, the clocks started again, with the freedom of their mistress.

Derian began again: 'Perfection? Oh yes, I too whispered to the sea girls and our sea people to take him down under the sand because of what he did to your poor sister, all calcified and twisted into threatening you with that bloody Nabob brush. The times I meant to tell her off! Not just your Nerys and Dilys took him down with a kiss (do not look shy boy, for they love you and warm you and you are more than one thing: that is how it is) but *many* of our girls, as they always did for the meanest of sailors. He was a bad man who hated the world and all in it. He hated love. Muted it, strangled it, killed it. I knew that he took her and there is more and you must be very brave for I need to awaken your memory'—and he took my hand.

I felt it.

Mammy.

Bronwen

Eleri.

'Where are they and what happened? Do you feel it, Almost?'

I sensed the big wave coming towards me, but at that moment a nurse came forward and touched me on the arm, saying that Derian was too unwell to talk further and they could see his agitation. He brushed my arm, still, and he said, 'What you felt, boy. It is a magic. I am old and dashed and paying for my land adventures, but still I am gifting to you this magic of ours. The sea—if it loves you and you are *of* it—will give you the power to influence and to compel. To shift in time and place; to sing and loose the voices in others, like you did with Myfanwy. Oh yes, I know of that, boy. I watched, I watched, but you already know that, even without the magic, round here thoughts carry and our landscape, on this coast, is breeding and alive. You feel it, as the willow at Clandestine spoke to you.'

He closed his eyes and I was ushered out.

I think that he lay in prison very ill, during the whole interval between his committal for trial and the coming round of the sessions or of his death, for I knew it was coming. He had broken two ribs, they had wounded one of his lungs when they arrested him because he had fought like a netted creature, instinct against his will, and now he breathed with great pain and difficulty, which increased daily and they say he had pneumonia, too. It was a consequence of his hurt body that he spoke so low as to be scarcely audible; though he spoke very little, what he said was on fire and he was ever ready to listen to me; and it became the first duty of my life to say to him, and sometimes read to him, what I knew he ought to hear and I knew that it was his duty, now, to say the same to me. Being far too ill to remain in the main part of the prison, he remained in the infirmary. This gave me opportunities of being with him that I could not otherwise have had. Had it been a different time, and but for his illness, I think he would have been put in irons, for he seemed to be regarded as a determined prison-breaker, a rough cat man that had no respect for authority and I know not what else. But they did not know, and how could they, that all was the thrashing of the sea creature hauled into captivity, and he could not help himself, then. Derian was, it is true, a wild man; the sea was his, but he wanted to explore the land and got into trouble, got into fights and was in the wrong place at the wrong time, keeping watch on my abominable father and then on me and on his landlocked daughter, whom he had never claimed because Miss Davies loved her and she was set for life, in a fine place on the Cleddau.

'Boy, forgive me for what I am. I wish I had been better. But there is more than one story that I am telling.'

Although I saw him every day, it was for only a short time; hence, the regularly recurring spaces of our separation were long enough to record on his face any slight changes that occurred in his physical state. I felt that I grew to know him well so quickly and it at once grew and broke my heart, for I understand what it was to have a father who loved you. Derian, well now he wasted, and became slowly weaker and worse, day by day, from the day when the prison door closed upon him. The kind of submission or resignation that he showed was that of a man who was tired out. I had an impression, from his manner or from a whispered word or two which escaped him, that he pondered over the question whether he might have been a better man under better circumstances. Perhaps, if he had stayed in the water and never cast off his sea garb, but he made no excuses for himself. It happened on two or three occasions in my presence, that his desperate reputation was alluded to by one or other of the people in attendance on him. A nurse; a prison officer. A smile crossed his face then, and he turned his eyes on me with a trustful look, as if he were confident that I had seen some small redeeming touch in him, even so long ago as when I was a little child. As to all the rest, he was humble and contrite, and I never knew him complain. And of course, he was right. He had watched us; cared for us and now he had bequeathed to me, both for my own good and so that I might at least try once more to win Seren and keep her in beauty and comfort.

When the Sessions came round, came Williams from his blasted Temple. He caused—and truly I could not tell if this were through kindness to Derian or just a need to be top-power, like—an application to be made for the postponement of his trial until the following Sessions. It was obviously made with the assurance that Derian could not live so long, and was refused. The trial came on at once, and, when the prisoner was put to the bar, he was seated in a chair. No objection was made to my getting close to the dock, on the outside of it, and holding the silvered hand that he stretched forth to me. Yes, silvered. You see, I looked so closely at that old hand and I saw that it had the silver marks of the sea scales on it, just delineated, for those who cared to see because they loved it so.

The trial was very short and very clear. Such things as could be said for him were said—how he had taken to industrious habits, and had thrived lawfully and reputably. Which was how how he had made money to be bequeathed to me, of course. But nothing could unsay the fact that he had returned, and was there in presence of the Judge and Jury. It was impossible to try him for that, and do otherwise than find him guilty. He had been found near the body of the old schoolmaster Llewhellin, dead in a mound of violets; there was money taken from The Sloop and he had been there, that night Perfection died; reports identified him and it made a pattern and I wanted to shout:

'He was watching for us! He is more to me than any father! And all these, these terrible hurts, they were by my own daddy, who so hated the world because some people do! It is easier, so much easier, to hate than to love! Hate is clear, crystal. It makes sense. But love, now that is not circular or linear and logical. You do not understand!'

Oh, what could I do? If it had been an earlier time, a Victorian time or the time of the last man hanged here in Swansea prison in 1958, I believe he would have gone to the gallows, for the indelible picture in my mind is of those sharp twelve men and women of the jury and I could scarcely believe, even as I say these words to you, that I saw twelve men and women say that, for all the things he stood convicted of, he would not leave; a life sentence. I hoped that he might get breath enough to keep life in him for what remained and what was still to tell to me. When I think of it now, the whole scene starts out in my mind again in the vivid colours of the moment, down to the drops of April rain on the windows of the court, glittering in the rays of sun on Oystermouth Road. He did not need to become convinced of his errors, because he knew what he had done wrong, but his right been much stronger and his sacrifice unspoken. He had sometimes yielded to passions in coming on land to quarrel and explore; he had left a haven of rest and beauty in the sea, and had come back to the country where he was proscribed and he stood convicted of the death of Llewhellin and of Perfection and other crimes of robbing and taking. The latter sometimes he had done and said so; the former never.

But they sentenced him and I called out. I wailed, 'No, it was Daddy!' and banged my hands on the wooden benches and hated the world. But Derian held my gaze steady and he said, 'I must prepare myself to die; in another time, they would have killed me, but I'm not long for the land world now.'

The sun was striking in at the great windows of the court, through the glittering drops of rain upon the glass, and it made a broad shaft of light between the twelve and the judge, linking both together, and perhaps reminding some among the audience how both were passing on, with absolute equality, to greater things. Rising for a moment, a distinct speck of face in this way of light, the prisoner called out for all to hear, 'More to me than any son!' and how I loved him as he sauntered out with a haggard look of bravery and nodded to the gallery. He had had to be helped from his chair, and to go very slowly; and he held my hand all this time and one of the jurors pointed at him and me and I stared hard and saw—sea magic—that she became dazed and that she faltered on her feet; this Derian saw and he took my wrist:

'Unless it is a matter of life and death, do not use your powers like that, bach.'

I earnestly hoped and prayed that he might die soon though there was more to say. I wanted to take him home and began to write out a petition to the Home Secretary, setting forth my knowledge of him, and how it was that he had come back for my sake, and for that of his lost daughter. I wrote it as fervently and pathetically as I could; and when I had finished it and sent it in, I wrote out other letters to such men in authority as I hoped were the most merciful, and drew up one to the Crown itself. I expect I was laughable, but I could not bear to let him go. I knew confinement must kill him. For several days and nights after he was sentenced I could not sleep, except when I fell asleep in my chair, but was wholly absorbed in these appeals. I would wake at dawn, in the blanket in which Rhys and Gwyneth has wrapped me. And after I had sent my passionate appeals in, I could not keep away from the cave where I had met him and I would roam the lanes and coast paths of an evening, and I would hover for the post. I had told them, the powers, that, while Derian told me himself of the bad things he had done, all the worse had been done by my father who was, I said, misplaced. But of course, what evidence did I have? Thoughts carry and the landscape speaks; to say where the old man was, the sea breathed to me and to my girls, but what is that in a court of law? And it did not matter: Derian would die. I wanted only his good name.

The daily visits I could make to Swansea prison were shortened now, and he was more strictly kept. Seeing, or fancying, that I was suspected of an intention of carrying poison to him, because Derian told those in the infirmary that he wished to go soon and by his own hand and that of those who loved him, I asked to be searched before I sat down at his bedside, and told the officer who was always there, that I was willing to do anything that would assure him of the singleness of my designs. Nobody was hard with him or with me, but they told me Derian was getting worse. He slept more, sometimes agitated even so. But there were kind windows. As the days went on, I noticed more and more that he would lie placidly looking at the white ceiling, with an absence of light in his face until some word of mine or thought brightened it for an instant, and then it would subside again. But before it did, the white ceiling was bathed in a pale blue and oh, girl, there was magic swirling. Sometimes he was almost or quite unable to speak, then he would answer me with slight pressures on my hand, and I grew to understand his meaning very well. And on a stronger day, he told me that he never wanted me to give up with Seren; to watch for her; he thought that Roland, who had chosen her for mastery, could not be forever, even so. And he told me that, at night, he was visited by my old family too.

You don't believe me?

Oh, but you must!

Derian brought alive the memories I had of Mammy, Bronwen and Eleri. Beauty; clacking teeth, too: those images the rattle-bag in my head, always. He told me that they swam away and I did not understand at first, but I hoped to, more. I had to wait, still.

It was ten days after the sentence when I saw a greater change in him than I had seen yet. His eyes were turned towards the door, and lit up as I entered; with that the pale blue light on the ceiling and the filigree reflection of gentle waves; soft sand; auger shells; brittle starfish; the lucent incarnadine anemone all so familiar even here, in this place where they hanged for the last time in Wales and so, 'Dear boy, Almost' he said, as I sat down by his bed: 'I trembled that you might be late. But then I knew you couldn't be that.'

'Never, Derian,' said I.

'Thank you dear boy, thank you. And you didn't desert me now.'

I pressed his hand in silence.

He lay on his back, breathing with great difficulty. Do what he would, and love me though he did, the light left his face ever and again, and a film came over the placid look at the white ceiling. Many times I thought he was gone. But, no. He seemed to fill up again, with a thought of something beyond Oystermouth Road and with indistinct whispers.

'Are you in much pain to-day?'

'I don't complain. But… your Seren came. And it is

different. I… told her, Almost. I told her I was her father. I… And her memory awoke.'

Seren. Always her. He bid her in his way and she heard him in her heart.

'It wasn't wrong, Derian. She is alone. The boy she came on land for and loved and hated; the man she married that she will never love and who cannot love and Miss Davies gone. She had to know. '

'And was she happy?'

But he seemed, finally, to have spoken his last words. He smiled, and I understood his touch to mean that he wished to lift my hand, and lay it on his breast. I laid it there, and he smiled again, and put both his hands upon it. Yes, she had been happy. As he told her, she recognised him as she lost him, tiny child. And she was strong, like Marina, as he cried, rent-heart, like Pericles, 'You are my child' and of how wild he was in his beholding. She took his hand. Now, I asked for a pillow as his breathing came heavy and I remembered more of the play and said (he smiled and I knew it had been him reading *Pericles* out at Clandestine House when I found the book, open-spined on the floor), 'And when you come ashore, I have a suit' and his heart only whispered, 'You shall prevail, were it to woo my daughter, For it seems you have been noble towards her.' It was as if she were with us now, each taking Derian's arm. *Exeunt.* And as he began to leave, though at first peaceful, I was seized with a powerful will to carry him from there and to the sea, but even if I could have done; if I could have found his garb, he would have been too tired.

The allotted visit time ran out, while we were thus; but, looking round, I found the governor of the prison standing near me, and he said softly, 'You needn't go yet, bach.' I thanked him gratefully, and asked, 'Can I still I speak to him, if he can hear me?'

The governor stepped aside, and beckoned the officer and the nurse away. The change, though it was made without noise, drew back the film from the placid look at the white ceiling, and he looked most affectionately at me.

'Dear Derian, if I talk to you now, will you understand what I say?'

A gentle pressure on my hand. I wanted to say these words, as I had confessed them to Miss Davies, though already he knew all:

'You had a child once, whom you loved and lost and she is safe though not where we would have her be.'

A stronger pressure on my hand.

'Seren. She is the most beautiful woman in the world and I love her! Keep that in your heart and you know it.'

With a last, or as I thought it was the last, faint effort, which might have been powerless but for my yielding to it and assisting it, he raised my hand to his lips. Then, he gently let it sink upon his breast again, with his own hands lying on it. On the white ceiling, came the pale blue light and the filigree lines, ripples in a rock pool on a warm day. I said,

'Bronwen and Eleri and Mammy. They left or were taken, they were buried, but are they at peace?'

He took my hand harder and gently pulled me to him and he said, 'Yes, Almost, and I am going to them now' and he closed his eyes and was still.

Still.

Or?

Then a commotion and shouting and hubbub all around.

Tiny creatures in motley shimmering rags in the ward, was it?

I knew in a heartbeat, then: my girls in land garb of the tiniest animals, mice and running: the rags, the sea garb, which they had found, I knew not how, but mermaids are not like us. Thoughts carry. Forms carry, for them. The sea garb touched his legs and he twitched. He had not been gone. The pale blue ceiling turned to navy and the land people were frightened, but I was not. Now Derian, sea magicked into a different land garb, transfigured, and breathing, though weak, a tiny creature, too. And all three gone from the window, holding tightly to a sea skin.

You're wondering how this can be true?

You don't believe me, but it is the very truth, though I am telling you more than one story. And we were headed all for Oystermouth Road, on the coast road and with a will even a weak creature can travel fast and so on to sea and if not safe then at peace. And I walked out of Swansea prison and the governor could not speak other than to say, 'I don't know what happened.'

And so I said, 'I saw nothing, Sir' but thought again of a very good description and added, 'I think a sea change sir. And into something rich and strange.' And also, to an audience which knew me not: 'I know where my mother is. Where all my blasted matriarchs are. They are under the sea. It wasn't your Derian Llewhellin who put them there, but my fiend of a daddy who didn't deserve the name. And that lad coughed up a burial that wasn't real and smiled through sad flowers, I am sure. But the sea will give up its dead and I know who will help me.'

And the man, he was a Chapel man, said I was besmirching *The Book of Revelation* 20:13 but I told him, 'Sir, you know nothing of revelation!' and I ran from that place and I called back what Derian's heart had told me: '"When you pass through the waters, I will be with you"—and that Sir is Isaiah 43:2!'

13

A cipher, not standing in rich place

I left the town, stifled in it, and went back to the headland. Out there, they swam; were gone. Nearby, the crabby man might still have been arguing about the statue of Amelia Earhart. Nothing had changed but everything had. Down I went to dawn to the sea cave; tide was in, but I could climb through to my own private beach and feel the cold spray warm me as I waited for more sea change. I remembered a poem my mother used to recite; still I don't know its provenance and it travelled like this:

I went out early, tiger-clad, for bravery's sake
To try the sea. Its bite was worse than mine—
It told harsh words and mumbles spat a briny sound
Of fury's heart. And I was spent, so roared no more.

I thought the sea would speak to me then, but it must not

have been time. I doubted myself and my very world: where were my sea girls? Derian? They did not come.

At this time, I, your Almost, was beginning to feel less than almost. I had Derian, a father, then he was gone; Seren lost to Griffiths, though her father had cradled his hopes of us together and I did not know if I could see Miss Davies again. Did not know if the crabbed spinster, now free, would want to come on land again. And to know what my own daddy had done to my sister, my matriarchs, in life and in death. To have taken a young woman, on her wedding day, and made her into a bride crone. And even to carry an understanding of that evil sorrow which had called Daddy to do what he had done—Oh, I felt such grief and that I would become a lesser extent of myself and, eventually, a cipher and not one standing in rich place.

It was at this time that I fell ill. In our time, we think we understand how sadness is created and of what it is composed. But we are only beginning to see how sadness, like the old melancholy, when felt to such a pitch, becomes intolerable and that is when our bodies break and the pain comes. Some days my legs were lead; I had tremors on one side. One night, all my starboard was weak as kittens and my port on fire. I see you are smiling at me, my strange argot, but I was all infected by the sea world! *I know, I know*. There was one time, though, in the driest land season by the sea storm, when I tried to stand and I could not. As Rhys and Gwyneth battened down the windows of our exposed headland home, one side of me was shivering; my arm and leg, electric and weak, my face in a one sided palsy, and they took me into the Withybush hospital then and I was sleeping and looked at when awake and they caressed my carotid artery and my head and chest with their machines, but my brains and all within me were as smooth as that of a child. Why then, was I so ill, amongst the acute cases of those held asleep and tiny bird-like ladies with their weeping grown men children who tried to make them speak and take their food?

I was sent home, weak and mewing; unable to stop the spittle from the corner of my mouth. I was Unexplained of Neurology in the end. Dr Morgan the Pints, he said so. But I knew it was the sadness, see? Miss Davies, free; Seren taken. Mammy, Bronwen, Eleri, all those good but brutal mothers, so beautiful; my troubled sister—and waiting for Derian and my girl who were yet to come and too ill to go back to my Dead Dears in Wiltshire.

I sent for book after book; bought endless things I did not need; sent Ned Owens more money for too much extravagance at the funerals he ran from our old house in Wiltshire, doing his paperwork in front of the fire under the coffin hatch. I said, 'Give them whatever they want, even the most opulent silk: ring up the King of Thailand for his tailor, if you want, boy. Line up posh coffins' and he did not argue with me because he was a soft heart and did not like to oppose. I said, 'Take your Anna-Katrina to town; take her away and spoil her boy because that is the sort of thing she likes. It would bring me pleasure. Decorate our house—chandeliers if you like!'—and so from my chair by the window. I made a tower of debt. We had money from Derian's bequest, but it was hardly endless and he had it held in instalments, sensible man.

I sat looking out at the water as the sea whipped and crêpey old Ishmael the Debts came for money because of what I had done. And Rhys soothed him; said, 'How is your sick wife, man?' and Ishmael croaked that she was too long alive and he wished for another with better limbs and hotter, ever, on the couch, but tidy with the lobster pots and always game out at sea, and Rhys said nothing back, in his modesty, to such flagrancy, but paid him what we could because there was no-one as careful with money as my brother in law. Then that man, my Rhys whom I had still not prized as I should, not bookish, like me, so he nursed me back to health slowly, slowly. I got stronger. Rhys spoke to Ned, told him I was reckless and to scale it back on the Dead Dears and any luxury there, like. Time moved slowly and twilight lasted all day, sometimes. Kind Gwyneth nursed me. I thought, sometimes, that I could fall in love with her; I had thought that in stray moments when I saw how she had cared so for my sister. But a sweep of a hand; a walk along the coast path; a love that was not ever burned by scorn. It was her and Rhys, see. They were in love, cleanly and neatly, and they would marry at Capel Dewi all crowned with the cowslips and primroses that I would gather from the hedgerows, when the time was right. That was their new beginning and I would bless it. I did not know what mine would be. Derian, Miss Davies free. Wondering if I should ever see them again; the unrest of my love for Seren and thinking of the poison that had been my own daddy, while I missed another who had loved and watched always.

Oh, don't cry, sweet listener! Your tears say that you are sorry for what happened; that you thought that for Almost it might be a new beginning, right away. Well now girl, I was coming to that. You see, to know when you are sad, you have to have known what happiness is. The child who has never been happy does not know he is sad and he may grow up all nasty, never free and light of heart. Full of a navy depth he cannot articulate. A pain that presses on him, but which he cannot describe. In my better moments, when I think of my father, this is how it went in my mind. He was repulsed by the world and wanted to expunge those in it, where he could, because it was revenge for his torment. Listen to me, girl. My lovely Catherine. It is a theory, alright. But I am telling you more than one story. You know that. Here is the other story, with magic you were yearning for. The first is mine—a sea tale; the second is yours, tired of life as you are, tired of cold indeterminate forms, the politics of a squalid summer and of all that you have told me: slights real and imagined; hearts rent—of all that has weakened and sucked the vigour of your spirits and made your sinews clamp up in tension.

But you know that you are sad because you felt happiness before, see?

14

A city's dead

So, you remember when I first came in and I said to you to listen? I know that when I ask this you will say, 'Almost, I always listen to you and for you, sleep or wake. And I am not the only one; of that I am sure.' That I'll reply, 'You're a top girl!'

But as I was saying, you recall my cast? My dead loves? Mammy. Dead, but it never makes any difference, does it? Bronwen Llewhellin, my grandmother. She's dead but extremely active and her teeth go clackety clack and she won't have them fixed because it's vanity? Eleri No-Name, my great grandmother. I said that the second bit of her, her *no-name*, was a mystery waiting for you to solve and also that though she was dead, she was never greater?

You said, before, 'Of course, I remember, though these Llewhellins are legion. Breeding like rabbits.' I laughed at that and said, '*Breeding*? Ah now, I would say it was more that they… diffuse. They move from where there are many to where they are few and so animate a world. I'm teasing you gently, but it is partly true.'

Now, girl, Look, see? Faces smile at you.

And out the back of your house are three faces, from elsewhere, or off-world.

Them. Oh yes. Come. Meet my matriarchs. They are not stopping because they have work to do, for others. Stories to tell.

The faces smile beatifically, grimace and gurn for fun: listen because they're addressing you! 'Hello, girl!' Bronwen's teeth rattled as she said that, a comic figure and she knows it; radiant. Mammy. Oh, I, Almost had not been exaggerating. She is beautiful enough to melt the heart of a star. Like Bronwen, there are little shells in her hair; delicate grey and iridescent periwinkles, polished up, almost; like the flank of a mackerel, an unexpected, dazzling thing; the wrack lies across her breast and she is briny and sea polished. You know it, don't you? You *feel it and felt it*. And Eleri. Flame hair; copper beauty. Perhaps you haven't solved her mystery but she is going to bid you to do so.

Don't you want to know? Where we came from, how we were buried in earth, but here?

Hear it, that shout from behind them: 'It's Evans the Bodies. I buried them these fine women but it was a strange thing. Light coffins. They were trimmed up elsewhere by Almost's daddy and some fellow in Pembroke he employed and I finished the job with a burial only out at Capel Dewi, but I was uncomfortable, see, with the boxes; I thought they were the wrong weight. I wasn't a courageous man in those days, see, before my Myfanwy sang like a bird and released the strength in me! I didn't challenge its strangeness or the odd look in that man's yellow eye… ' and he had gone, puff, to tell his story elsewhere and love his Dead Dears back at the milking parlour.

'Listening, proper, like?' (Eleri speaks to you.) 'you see Bronwen went first, then Almost's mammy, all gone and thought out to sea, from the sea cave after a walk, or caught by the tide, mired by a fall and washed out and I had this idea because they knew the sea and its moods and none of it made sense girl, that it was a dark magic and that if I took away my name, my Llewhellin, so many deaths, us, then somehow I could hide who I was. I was scared, see. They were taken out to sea and I thought it was a curse, like. *Some thing*, Celtic magic, a shape-shifter, came to them and spoke magic to compel them under the water. But you know there was no magic in *his* rough hands, only a slouching beast. Someone who had never been happy or free and who hated our spirit.'

'Yes listener.' (Now Mammy speaks to you and can see that your expression tells, *Oh God, she is aflame with it*) 'Daddy. That man. He took and he took and he plunged us under and we breathed water for a while and then not. It was all revenge for the world he hated and even when he was alive he robbed us of our goodness.'

And you are thinking, '*But here now*?' aren't you girl?

'Well now'—Bronwen speaks, clackety-clack; and hears

you though you did not speak aloud—'I am not saying we are *alive* exactly, but does it matter, girl, that sort of thing? Not in our parts, does it heaven and hell. But we were raised up and free from the places where Daddy had trashed us over his bad boat. And a merman came to us and he loved Mammy especially and he spoke the magical *englynion*, a sea poem, and we were raised up from the sea to live with him and with his kind. And with him, those two beautiful girls who so caressed Almost, your Nerys and Dilys and they sends their regards, Almost, you hot boyo!'

Eleri now: 'We have things to do. Thoughts carry. See, Mammy knows she was too harsh on Perfection and too rough on Almost, but it was her unhappiness, with Daddy see. Almost understood it in the end. And to look at it with fresh eyes, perhaps if your name was Perfection, in the end you has to try. And when he hurt her, as he did, she did a thing of uncommon beauty. She could have called for the sea and we could have helped, but she did not. She chose to propel Rhys into the future and a life with Gwyneth, for she knew that it was Gwyneth Rhys truly loved. That is a thing of perfection, although it is tragic. She had the sadness; she did not want to give herself up to the sea freedom, but to be laid to earth. And as for boy, here, well now, what's wrong with that name—with *Almost*? Because when you get *there*, there is no there, and *Almost* is a glimpse of the perfection that looks a bit shaggy-like close up, see? I knows I don't express myself well, girl.'

'Right. Come on Miss Davies, Aeres, girl! Time to go!' Ah, there's more company here.

Of course, in her land garb, with that of the sea in her pocket-book. Taken at the point of death and probably more alive than this company but, as they said and as you are learning, girl, it doesn't really matter, does it?

And Mammy: 'I have a poem I wrote once for Miss Davies, don't you know. Oh I know all about Daddy and her. I didn't when I married him and she was too enclosed in her dark suffering to say, but now she is my friend and we might even laugh about that dreadful spider cake one day and how her pain infected the world about and made the moss creep across the foot of any *parasit*. Yes, Almost, we hope it'll suck down Williams, one day! In the sea, when you are stymied by your darkness, your sadness, then comes a fresh tide to blow you clean. It cannot happen so on land and that is why we have our stories and, as Almost has told you, thoughts travel once the sea has breathed its magic and, perhaps, the hand of Derian Llewhellin has brushed your arm and your edges are blurred. This is what I wrote for the keeper of Clandestine House. I called her the Madonna of the Cleddau. And I would say,

The sea coast was too far for you;
to keep inland was your advice,
away from Jack Tar, foreign folk:
Stay cloistered on this estuary.
Madonna of the Cleddau, come:
square jaw, dark eyes and, counterpoint,

retroussé nose and powdered cheeks:
and born of earth, not briny downs
the shutters down, the tapers lit,
and trapping Seren with claw hand,
then plaintive songs of field delight.
But, round the wall, the blue began,
spoke not to you: you had no thought
to jump and best a warmer wave;
a voyage out was lost on you.
what did you care for *them* or *theirs*?
Madonna's night world of the quay
had supernatural force: the owls,
the rustle of the hawk, black elms,
the screech and call and *elsewhere* sound.
Such pale wings drew on navy sky
as you looked out across the flats
and thought that this was world enough,
the kelp, the wrack was only stench.
Madonna of the Cleddau, *mine*:
I sing to you from farther shores:
I tell you of my odyssey—
we could have basked it, you and I.
Sea always changed, waves' thunderous moods
could not be captained, made anew.
I see Clandestine now and wish
the sea would roar and cry and break
the weeded walls, the altered beds,
bring kelp and shells to bruise the stones

where mortar tidily restrains.
A sea breeze, green thunder and a changed world.

And now they are gone. With Miss Davies and Evans the Bodies, to do what they must do and could and I, Almost, recall this. That I went back to Clandestine and as it happened, the sea *did* roar and cry and break the weeded walls, the altered beds; brought kelp and shells to bruise the stones where mortar tidily restrained. Because, round here, poems carry. Don't cry, Catherine. It is a good thing and it may have been a shock to be pressed in upon by ghostly faces, but we need to tug at the seams of this world sometimes. To see what lies. To find the rapture.

15

Roar, cry and alter

I was torn, bisected and still thinking of Seren. Enclosed out at Clandestine House. Oh, the light that could always surround that scornful beauty. She outshone any other beauty. Proud, inflexible and taught to be that way. She made my heart ache and ache again; when last I saw her she had lamented and refused to see me. When she met her father again, she had written to me and so it went:

Dear Almost,

I went to the Swansea prison and I met Derian. You will know what occurred. Since then, I cry but I know that, though he died to the world maybe, he is free and of the sea and with your girls. Oh yes: you think I did not know of them? I know all seaways and that I was lost to them but felt them and I would always suffer because you, though you did not mean it, destroyed me, though a boy, by making me follow your voice onto land. It was love and it will always be but I hate you for it and will always scorn you and I know this is a paradox hard to tolerate. All other men I can deceive and entrap. At night, when Roland snores, perhaps I will continue to do so though I may be called a whore. And as for him, though I suppose I entrapped him with what you think is my beauty (and I know I have it and will use because this is what I was taught at Clandestine House), my punishment is that I am trapped by a man, successful in Pembrokeshire, but a boor and a dullard. He has no imagination, he has no heart, and does not see or feel the things that you or I could but he has given me wealth and status and I suppose that these things are good and useful, though not free and clearly of earth not water.

It was at this point that I made myself stop reading. I cannot adequately express to you what pain it gave me to think of her with Roland Griffiths. Of her, laid up on linen with that man. How she could have shown any favour to a contemptible, sulky, misanthrope, so far below the average, but elevated in status and with riches beneath his feet and a gilded cage for her; a dark net about her starlight. I hated to think of her flattering him; in the bed; at a ball; over dinner. It was intolerable. But, just as Derian had given her up in the thought that her life might be better—and out of kindness to a splinter-hearted spinster—so, through love, I had done the same. I knew that I reminded her of what she might have been; I had wrested her from the sea, to be raised, hating the land world, by a broken-hearted claw hand. And yet, Miss Davies, at the point of death, was liberated: they must have found, my girls, her sea garb, and dressed her in it and made her free. Could it not yet be possible for Seren? As I told you, at the beginning, of the mermaids and mermen—indulge me to tell more now?—so, 'in possessing an amphibious nature, they are enabled not only to exist in the ocean, but to land on some rock, where they frequently lighten themselves of their sea-dress, resume their proper shape, and with much curiosity examine the nature of the upper world belonging to the human race. Unfortunately, however, each merman or merwoman possesses but one skin, enabling the individual to ascend the seas, and if, on visiting the abode of man, the garb be lost, the hapless being must unavoidably become an inhabitant of the earth.'

But I was saying about Seren's letter to me. She had continued,

It is too late, but perhaps, at some time, we can see each other again. By the sea. Find me. You will know where and choose the day. But I can bear my pain, for what does it matter? How should anything matter? You remember those early days at Clandestine House when she would send to Perfection for young Almost? Miss Davies wanted your spontaneity; the fire and possibility she saw in you while her heartbreak, as you understand it now, made her loathe the world and made her create me to break hearts, including, as you see, my own. Yes, I do know that it was your daddy that broke her own heart before he courted your mammy and did evil to them all. And thoughts carry; whispers of the sea tell me things, still, and I know, Almost, what you have done with that trembling power which Derian Llewhellin passed on to you: I know your daddy is under the silt and I see now what Miss Davies was and what she gave up, for me, to stay on land and even grow wary of the sea because she could not return, cloistered on the estuary, for my sake and because she was locked up with her bitterness and that wretched wedding feast with its nasty spiders and creeping mould.

I shudder when I think about it all. That clock stopped at the time her heart broke and she was killed, in time; the darkness and the tapers and the silver salvers so beautiful against the gloom and the dust. Depredation! And you came and I scorned you. I said, at the door, nothing more than, 'You are to come this way' and I looked you up and down because your dress and manners were poorer than mine and you were ashamed. You did not know that you had put me in this place. 'Go over there boy and stay until you are wanted,' I said and smirked and again you saw, and then when you saw Miss Davies and she told you, 'Come here! Play, boy!'

There were other guests then; people creeping after her money, flattering her—but in you, though, just a boy. I saw only kindness and something else too: you were special, Almost. And I knew later, from Derian, my father (and I say this aloud to make myself believe it now), that you would have taken and bested a kind of magic. Storytelling, but the ability to move freely, in time; to loose a voice. Oh yes, I know of Muffled Myfanwy; and I know of how my father watched over you not just for my sake but because he grew to see you as his son. And as for Miss Davies, now she grew to love you too. She sent for you because she knew of the

Llewhellins of course and heard that you were an odd bookish child, spending long hours on the beach: she thought you would be interesting, but the love she did not expect. I think it began that day when, with the flatterers around her—'How well you look!'; 'And as for that dress!'; 'You are blooming Miss Davies!'—she cried out, 'None of these things are true! I am yellow skin and bone!' and there was nothing the oily visitors could say, but you, Almost, crept forward and placed your hand on the bent back and said, 'But Miss Davies, I like you how you are!' and the clawed hand raked your back and she shook as she wept because you were a true thing; an honest thing. Almost, cariad, that is who are you.

We quarrelled so badly; I expect you guessed. I told her I hated her and that she had caged me, though she loved me. And I spat at her; in my life I was trapped twice. By you; by her. Now again, with Roland, but that is what must be because I cannot return to the sea. I told Miss Davies that her schooling had ruined me because I learned only confinement and to fear the world and its beautiful daylight, while in my blood, the pale blue and the navy of the sea world ran ripples. It is a source of such anguish to me. Derian, I hope, will come to see me. And to you. I think that there are others you will see, if you have not already. Perfection, I think, lies in earth. As I said, one day we might see each other again. Find someone, Almost, to love. And go to the Cleddau to see the house; there is something necessary for you there.

Kind listener, this is how it was. And the wasting away and recklessness I felt were really all for her. That woman filled my heart from the moment I saw her, and so often made it ache and ache again and how I wish she could have been free and that her baby intelligence had not received its first powerful distortions from Miss Davies's wasting hands and that she had not been lost because of me. And there had been many old books at Clandestine House, though little did I see them read. As I understood more of the place, I supposed that maybe they entertained worlds Miss Davies and Seren could not bear to enter. Like the book open with its spine breaking I told you about earlier: it was *Pericles*, girl. And I knew now that Derian had been reading it and that was how we spoke of Marina, the lost daughter. Another book, mouldering on the sideboard, was *Tales of the Genii*, referred to by some old authors as, an *Eastern Story*. It is pertinent to how I felt. Pertinent to how Miss Davies felt before her world crashed in, at two o'clock, when time stopped in Clandestine House. In that Eastern story, the heavy slab that was to fall on the bed of state in the flush of conquest was slowly wrought out of the quarry, the tunnel for the rope to hold it in its place was slowly carried through the leagues of rock, the slab was slowly raised and fitted in the roof, the rope was slowly taken through the miles of hollow to the great iron ring. All being made ready with much labour, and the hour come, the sultan was aroused in the dead of the night, and the sharpened axe that was to sever the rope from the great iron ring was put into his hand, and he struck with it, and the rope parted and rushed away, and the ceiling fell. So, in my case; all the work, near and afar, that tended to the end—which is to say a time in which I might be free and continue to do things of importance and that time in which my confidence grew—had been accomplished; and in an instant the blow was struck, and the roof of my stronghold dropped upon me.

What could I do? Crawl out; to the house.

I went. Clandestine House was in a dusty ruin of beached wrack.

This was what Seren had thought necessary. I had to see it, for me to leave this place now that it had fallen, now that it was reclaimed, and, so, leave my time here and my heart.

The gardens in which my girls, Dilys and Nerys, sometimes took land form to watch over their boy, were ever more decrepit. The ruins. Well now, I would say it was a fire, but that is not quite how it was; the stones, plants and paths; the old brass lantern over the door, the living breathing house and all around it had died. The willow that had revealed my father's name entwined with his wretched bride to be had cracked and peeled and wept; the moss that crept was desiccated and not fed from the hungry underground springs. I felt that, with her gone, the house could not breathe. And yet… around the quay, were new people. From away, I suppose. It was as if they could not see the mouldering suffering house and all around it. *As if they could not see me*, a crying spectre of a man in a ghost house. These people, they were putting up their substantial lives with their cheerful bunting at the pub, The Clandestine Arms, on the quay. Lawns were manicured and doors trimmed up in grey-green all tasteful like, not our old, old polished wood, a copper or russet paint with the spyhole, just in case. As I said, I am telling you more than one story: one is yours; one is mine, but there is a third and I suppose it is this: how do you tell, when you come from a storied landscape, what is alive and what is dead? What is really there and what was only intended, presumed spoken into being? Can you tell? Who am I? Did you make me, or am I really just so? The lad from the sea cliff, from the turbulent Llewhellins, that you call up, in the sad, dry season you find yourself in now?

Ah. Your Almost smiles at you. You are not sure. Good. *To be sure closes doors.*

Now listen more. There's a poet I loved, as Evans the Bodies loved Herbert—you remember?—a Welsh priest man but of the North. R.S. Thomas he was and I met him once, over a grave, and he did the man proud with his resonances. Listen now and, when I am gone, hold a shell in your hand. Go to the headland, the cleft cliff or the quay. Find an auger and then, still yourself and listen, like he says, in his *Prayer*. Oh now, don't cry girl. You are safe.

What was the shell doing,
on the shore? An ear endlessly
drinking?
What? Sound? Silence?
Which came first?
Listen.

16

A star descends. The end, is it?

Now girl, if you wouldn't mind making tea and trimming up some Welsh Cakes but without a recipe and with one hand only, I shall offer you my last. Do you know, that sometimes stories have two endings? Of course you do. In old books, sometimes the author wrote an ending that was too sad and his publisher demanded it more palatable; a triumph. Triumph is sometimes untrue, of course, but what would you like? What do you expect? So here is how it might have gone.

Seren.

Scorn.

Star.

The most beautiful thing that ever walked on land or swam in sea.

Oh, now te. *Look, so.* Bake on. We have more guests, though I do not know if they will come in as they'll surely have work to do.

Derian. More to me than any father. There he is at your window.

My girls, Nerys and Dilys. Oh, too hot, too hot!

And they beam at us and I think that, at your sleeve, you felt a hand though you had not seen him come in. Edges blurred when Derian Llewhellin brushed your arm, as I can hope he did. Now, I see that you are crying, happy, and the squalid summer blows in an azure breeze and up comes a splash of tar and the night world of the quay. The anemone and the brittlestar and the pinching crab; the auger shell of Perfection which I'd told you about; the boat ride out from St Justinian and the freedom found somewhere between rock and rock. Derian and the girls kiss their Almost—they full-mouth kiss you, oh gorgeous—and are gone. The sea light, ripples, doesn't it? Dazzling. It is, almost, too fine to tolerate… and then this is what I say to you: Now, te. The two endings. Listen and choose. I begin with a poem. For her. Seren. *Everything is for her.*

If I should fall, then say to me the reason waves form as they are,
Why ice should seed along a scratch, why I should love my six point star.
I do not know or care to see the smiles that fall in brazen line,
But innocence and clearest eye embolden me to make her mine.
I speak of love and quiet worlds, the county town on winter nights:
The sweets of honey bees, a view of ruby sky and amber

lights—
A mermaid Terpsichore, sand-snow, auroras made of rosy glow,
My Borealis blood red sheen—if I should fall, then make me know.
When I am not and you are here, beholden to this dusty room,
Be gentle with the tenuous forms of memory; do not grieve too soon.
Consider this—why should we be, ephemeral and urgent? How?
And speak to me with confidence, declaim for me on cliff or prow.
In nature's fragile frame I see a world that lives beyond the hill,
Beyond the log pile, salt and shed; behind our eyes when we lie still.
And when I fall, then say to me you read sea language, pure and keen—
And set my records on my desk and light my lamp: make them be seen.

I met her out there. *I felt her*, thoughts carry: I always knew where she was. I walked beyond St David's to look at the Blue Lagoon, turned back and walked and walked to Abereiddy, then through the bluebell wood, by the mud and stream to the fierce mouth, Abermawr. Skimming stones into the sea, she was. Oh God, aflame. I could hardly stand her beauty. She saw me and walked slowly my way as I cupped a pebble and steadied my thoughts and tried to control my tears.

Seren. Star. *Always her.* A mermaid I trapped on land and who never forgave me.

She said this: 'Boy. Always boy.'

I said, 'Age does not wither her' I could never be lying and because I looked on her I saw I was fresher and new, still.

'Roland is dead. I am… I am different, Almost.'

Oh she wept and howled into and out of a fierce mouth and hurled the rocks across the breakers and I went to her and held her while she told me of her life with him; of the spite that held, the jokes that cracked and broke; resentments, brutal, scorning others just because they had a better boat, a finer cast of house or leg or anything. He hated the world and everyone in it, handsome damned man who had fooled her. I said, 'I will find him dead and flay him for you, Seren, for you, my love' and I meant it, hating brute like Daddy, down under the sand in another sea and time. My howl was elemental; perverse. We clung to each other.

He, Roland, touched her wrong; he did not cradle her at night, not understand that her own beautiful scorn was from her pain, sea girl trapped, and if he had, what would it have mattered? He had her to set on his arm and place where he should and that was enough. He used her roughly; cursed her barren; not a mother, nor a soft gentle thing. He cast her out, within her home. I could not stand to hear it all and howled again and she clung and my God I cannot tell you how beautiful she was because it would be like… it would be like trying to beat the heart of a star with a warped broom; like lifting up prayers with dirty hands and biting mouths. That is something like it was.

We walked out through the woods and I gathered bluebells, pressed them upon her in a fever.

'Forgive me, Almost.'

'I already have,' I said; I fell on my knees in the stream and mud and the bluebells were crushed with I and her and us together, tremendous.

Her heart was opened then. I saw it.

Afterwards, I took her hand and I knew that there would be no shadow of another parting from her. I thought, also, that one day we might find her garb, as for Derian out at Oystermouth; as for Miss Davies, somewhere in her wild garden, under the fingers of creeping moss and the care of the kind willow. With the prompt of the ever-changing house that was alive. There might, yet, be a way back to the sea. *For her, for Seren*—and in growing magic or the charms of the englynion, because poems carry, for me.

17

Or a star dies

But then again, is this how it was? Catherine, do you prefer this ending?

I begin, as I often do, with a poem. This one is about endings, when we come to recognise they have arrived, that is. So,

We climbed the downward spiral of the trail
To best the shedding fingers of the cliff;
I'd promised you, oh love, I could not fail—
I'd prove to you against our childish tiff
That there was treasure to be found that day—
Albescent moons to cradle in your hand—
Sea urchins fine, a little world to say:
Echinocardium, wanting to be grand.
But my world was not yours, you did not care
To hold the little lanterns in your palm—

The hollow globe within the greatest fair,
You did not care if such should come to harm.
So cracked the sea potato on the tide:
I knew, although I smiled, my love had died.

I knew where she was. *I felt her*. I walked there, out beyond St David's, the lovely harbour at Abereiddy, turquoise of the Blue Lagoon, then through the bluebell woods to Abermawr. She knew I would find her, of course. Out there, hurling stones across the breakers and howling her pain. She did not stop me taking her in my arms, drawing time-stopping kisses from her. Too late, too late, though.

For this is what happened.

Everything I said of Roland was true, but when he died, consumed by his own acid and pride, Seren married a quiet local man. Not rich, but comfortable, like, and they lived in a house looking out across Ramsey Sound. This is the road she had taken, my beautiful mermaid girl. And she had a child, too: how could I claim her now? Oh listener, do not laugh: she called the boy 'Nearly' and he was her joy. I could see that. How could I claim her now? She seemed old, though she was not, and greatly changed and sad, but never, I tell you, could custom stale the infinite variety of this miraculous woman.

What could I do? My heart was broken.

I reached down and picked up an auger shell, she cupped it in her hand with tears in her eyes and then she turned, picking her way across the pebble beach to the bluebell wood and she was gone.

And that is the ending, almost. Which ending did you prefer? Which shall we have? And really, all I want to ask you, is this: did any of this happen? Was any of it true? And am I really here, on a knowing day of the year and in your kitchen. Now, what do you think?

Then I, well of course I wept, cried until I was dry, not comprehending the world. I felt his fingers brush my arm: electric. Then he was gone, too, and had ended his story.

Acknowledgements

For my husband, Ned, his hand in mine; my boys, Elijah, Isaac and Caleb: love forever. To Becketts and Llewhellins; for Wales and especially Pembrokeshire; for the family that was born but, and never more so, for the family that was made: my friends; for you, our neighbours; community; our children. Especially for Alexi and Susie; for the support of Alex Campbell, Kate Armstrong, Heidi James and Avril Joy. Then for Patricia Borlenghi, Sarah Howe and Emma Kittle-Pey.

An extract from chapter one was published in *New Welsh Reader*, May 2018.

Bibliography

The poems you see here and there are my own; a pamphlet I wrote called, *Thalassa Môr*, the two words being Greek and Welsh, respectively, for sea. The poem in chapter 4 was previously published in The Emma Press's *Anthology of the Sea.* Almost Llewhellin wrote the epigraph, 'Lewis'. You can see he did. Catherine's paraphrased quotation in the first and last chapters, 'we had nothing before us…' is from chapter one of Charles Dickens's *A Tale of Two Cities.* Williams the lawyer quotes from the beginning of Ben Jonson's play, 'Volpone'. 'No Man is an Island' does not, of course, come from *The Mabinogi* (whose stories I draw on lightly throughout), but from John Donne, 'MEDITATION XVII, Devotions upon Emergent Occasions': to me this feels painfully prescient, bearing in mind the political decisions made in this country of late which, in themselves, inspired me to take refuge in this strange little book.

'No man is an Iland, intire of itselfe; every man
is a peece of the Continent, a part of the maine;
if a Clod bee washed away by the Sea, Europe
is the lesse, as well as if a Promontorie were, as
well as if a Manor of thy friends or of thine

owne were; any mans death diminishes me,
because I am involved in Mankinde;
And therefore never send to know for whom
the bell tolls; It tolls for thee.'

A line that describes Almost's sister, Perfection, is from Donne's poem, 'The Anagram':

'Though all her parts be not in th' usual place,She hath yet an anagram of a good face.'

Marina is the lost daughter of Pericles, in Shakespeare's eponymous play, which is referred to in this book and which, it transpires, Derian has been reading. And the quotations come from scene 21. (The play, its full title, 'Pericles, Prince of Tyre', is a reconstructed one and organised only into scenes, not acts.) I have always found the way Shakespeare handles the theme of lost things found almost intolerably moving; here and most of all, in my favourite play, 'The Winter's Tale'. The reference to the 'Eastern Story' is from *Great Expectations* and I have used part of the text in my description of Almost's 'stronghold' falling, as it falls for Pip when he meets Estella again and hears her vehemently and unapologetically account for her ability to entrap men while she dances around the coarse, dull Drummle at a ball. This, Pip cannot bear. All other brief quotations will I hope be forgiven as fair useage.

Landscape

Although this is a work of fiction, I have woven in real places because the parts of the country concerned are intrinsically part of me and jostle to be in any story I might want to tell. Most of the book is set on or around St Brides Bay, Pembrokeshire and also around St David's Head and inspired by the beautiful woods and water on the sea coast and inland, on the Stackpole estate. Capel Dewi is based on the church at Walton West, above Broad Haven, wherein legions of my my family are buried. There again, Bethesda church, towards Tenby. Pop, my great grandparents. Storied landscapes. The house in Wiltshire, with its coffin hatch, is based on my own home. And as for the funerals, the embalming, the living poltergeist landscape, ah: bedtime stories, gone deep. Stories my grandmother told me.

An explanation of the two endings

Because of the mystery and ambiguity of the book, the uncertainty of its endings, or rather that Catherine, the kind listener, and you, as reader should have some choice in how it ends, seemed fitting to me. But there is another reason. *The Life of Almost* recalls how *Great Expectations* had its ending changed at the last moment. Edward Bulwer Foster, Dickens's friend and a fellow novelist, had been keen to see that Pip and Estella were united at the end of the story, whereas in the original version they were not. The account goes that Dickens felt his friend argued such a good case that he subsequently agreed to make a change. 'I resolved... to make the change... I have put in as pretty a little piece of writing as I could and I have no doubt the story will be more acceptable through the alteration.' George Bernard Shaw published an edition of *Great Expectations* in a limited edition run with his preferred ending: the one Dickens had written first and which he argued was, in fact, 'the truly happy ending.' Some have argued that this was a perverse argument, but I prefer the sobriety of the original and find it more fitting for the brooding, disillusioned narrative tone through the book. So, for interest's sake, here are the two:

'I took her hand in mine, and we went out of the ruined place; and, as the morning mists had risen long ago when I first left the forge, so the evening mists were rising now, and in all the broad expanse of tranquil light they showed to me, I saw no shadow of another parting from her.'

OR, the former, when Pip, walking along Piccadilly, is told a lady in a carriage wishes to speak to him: it is Estella:

'…I was very glad afterwards to have had the interview; for, in her face and in her voice, and in her touch, she gave me the assurance, that suffering had been stronger than Miss Havisham's teaching, and had given her a heart to understand what my heart used to be.'

But it is time for Almost:

'But now, if you wouldn't mind making tea and trimming up some Welsh Cakes but without a recipe and with one hand only, I shall offer you my last. Do you know that, sometimes, stories have two endings? *Of course you do.* In old books, sometimes the author wrote an ending that was too sad and his publisher demanded it more palatable; a triumph. Triumph is sometimes untrue, of course, but what would you like? What do you expect and how may I help? And yet,

A grave at Capel Dewi, Broad Haven: *In Loving Memory of Almost Derian Llewhellin of Druidstone Haven. Presumed lost at sea, with his beloved wife, Seren Davies Llewhellin, of Clandestine Quay, May 1963.'*

About the author

Anna Vaught is a novelist, essayist, poet, editor, reviewer and also a secondary English teacher, tutor, mental health campaigner and mother of three sons. She runs the Fabian Bursary, offering one to one teaching for disadvantaged young people interested in the arts. This novella is the second title published by Patrician Press. The first was *Killing Hapless Ally,* an autobiographical novel about mental health problems. Her next book, a work of historical fiction, *Saving Lucia*, will be published in 2020 by Bluemoose; she is currently working on her fourth novel, *The Revelations of Celia Masters*, and collaborating on a mixed anthology. Her blog is www.annavaughtwrites.com. Follow her on twitter @bookwormvaught

#0023 - 260718 - C0 - 216/138/11 - PB - 9781999703028